So That You Can Know Me

An Anthology of Pakistani Women Writers

GARNET WORLD FICTION

So That You Can Know Me

An Anthology of Pakistani Women Writers

Edited by
**Yasmin Hameed &
Asif Aslam Farrukhi**

UNESCO Collection of Representative Works

So That You Can Know Me
An Anthology of Pakistani Women Writers

Published by
Garnet Publishing Limited
8 Southern Court, South Street
Reading, Berkshire, RG1 4QS, UK

UNESCO Publishing
1 rue Miollis
75732 Paris Cedex 15, France

UNESCO Collection of Representative Works
The publication of this work was assisted by a contribution of the Islamic
Republic of Pakistan under UNESCO's Funds-in-Trust Programme

Translations from the Punjabi, the Pushto, the Seraiki,
the Sindhi and the Urdu

ISBN 1 85964 114 8

UNESCO Collection of Representative Works
UNESCO ISBN 92 3 103433 2

First UK Edition 1997

British Library Cataloguing-in-Publication Data
A catalogue record for this book is available from the British Library

Jacket and book design by David Rose
Typeset by Samantha Abley

Printed in Lebanon

Contents

Munni *Bibi* Goes to the Fair

Hajra Masroor

The flickering flame of the torch – and the sound of drum and harmonium: the crows nesting in the trees of the spacious court-yard got caught up in the branches as they restlessly fluttered their wings. For a second she tinkled her anklet-bells melodiously, then sang on. When she reached the last note of the song, a turmoil set in – the drum-beater jerked his head and jumped up and down beating the drum; the harmonium player, trying to keep pace with the frenzy, ran his fingers swiftly over the keys; while the poor torch-bearer stood there the whole. After singing the verse, the dancer spun round and round frantically inside the circle of spectators, moving her feet to the rhythm, flashing in and out of sight like lightning so swiftly that the torch-bearer had great difficulty keeping her face within the circle of light. He, poor soul, also had to take care, lest the fluttering flame scorch the dancer. The wretched torch was actually a mud-splattered kerosene bottle which had to be tilted this way and that to keep it blazing.

Munni *Bibi*, half-dozing and cuddled up in Kamal's lap, watched the dancing, swinging flame and the dancing, swinging woman.

She had almost fallen asleep when Kamal had picked her up and brought her out to watch the spectacle.

Munni *Bibi* was totally enthralled by the dancing flame and the dancing woman, against the dark, dreary night but she really wanted to sit cross-legged and upright on the ground like the boys and the rest of the servants of the neighbourhood to watch the show. Like the others, she wanted to lift her hand to touch the swirling skirt and try to get under its umbrella-like swirl. But no one could do that anyway, because the dancer's movements were so swift that the torch-bearer actually had to run after her in order to bring her back into the spotlight, whereupon she would once again start sparkling afresh. The tinsel and diamanté jewellery stitched on to the dark purple *dupatta* draped over her head and bosom – the wide swirl of the green skirt contrasting with the tightly fitted green pyjamas – all glittered as though on fire. In the glow of the torch, her silver earrings, silver head-adornments and the golden necklace all kept swinging round her face. The silver-belled bangles jingled as she tried to push away the supposedly heartless lover with the rhythmic, graceful movements of her arms, hidden under long, draping sleeves.

Munni *Bibi* gave the woman the coins that Kamal had slipped to her. The woman leapt forward flirtatiously, took the money and, after showering her affection on the little girl, receded to croon the melodious song once again.

Watching, dazed, Munni enjoyed herself so much she grew magnanimous enough to sympathize with her sisters, who were pestering Kamal for more coins. She offered one of the coins to her sister so that she too could do as she wished. Her attention was caught by the upright, unmoving trees in the dim glow. She looked for the spirits in the trees which her nanny had prattled on about, but could find no sign of them. Behind the dancing light of the torch, the trees looked taller than ever before, so high that their tops seemed to merge with the sky.

Resting her head on Kamal's shoulder, she heard a row flare up between Kamal and the plump servant of the neighbours, but, not understanding what it was about, she fell into a deep slumber.

The next day when her father returned from visiting another town, the plump servant waylaid him to complain about Kamal, and her father's rage knew no bounds. He came into the house shouting at Kamal.

Kamal was a servant and yet not a servant. He had been raised and brought up in Munni's house since childhood. Although he drew pay from the government hospital, he was in mortal fear of Munni's father.

"How dare you invite troupes in my absence and expose the womenfolk of my house to this trash! You must have spent at least two rupees on her! Is this how you squander your money?"

Pulling hard on Kamal's ears, her father kept on scolding. Her mother pleaded with him, trying to convince him for the millionth time that none of the ladies had watched the show. They had only taken the tiniest peep through the chinks of the door.

In spite of being beaten and thrashed, Kamal stood his ground and denied having anything to do with the troupe, insisting that the fat servant had in fact arranged it all and was wrongly implicating him in the whole business.

Munni *Bibi* burst into tears. Kamal was punished and grounded for twenty-four hours. The rule was that, until he got married, he was supposed to come straight back to the house on returning from duty at the hospital and was not supposed to venture out again.

Munni *Bibi* could not bear to see the hot flushed face of Kamal. Fleeing away from the scene, she went outside where her sisters and the neighbourhood children had gathered. They frightened Munni by saying that all those who had given coins to the dancer would be punished in hell by having red-hot coins plastered over their bodies.

"Thank God! I only gave one coin! May God forgive me!" said Munni *Bibi*'s sister complacently, consoling herself that she would be spared much of the agony.

Munni Bibi grew deeply agitated. Her grief at Kamal's plight turned into a throbbing rage. How she regretted her folly. She remembered once being told by her aunt from Lucknow that dancing and such frolics would be considered sins on the Day of Judgement. After a little while, dragging her mother's dirty *dupatta,* she went to Kamal's quarters.

"Teach me to say my prayers, Kamal," she said, turning her face away to make it clear to him that she was talking to him only through dire necessity.

"Why? This is not prayer time," growled Kamal.

"I have to atone for the sin that I committed," Munni *Bibi* sobbed.

"What sin!" Kamal sat upright on the bed.

"You made me give her the money." She dissolved into tears. "Now I'll be burnt in hell-fire."

"Oh, Little One! God will never burn you. I'll tell Him to burn me instead – okay?"

And Munni *Bibi* dried her tears. She knew that Kamal always kept his word to her.

As the season changed, Munni *Bibi* fell ill. After a fortnight's fever she became so irritable and grumpy that even Kamal was unable to make her smile. Her nanny became her sole confidante. Cool with everyone else, she pestered the nanny with endless questions about God – what did He look like? Did He like children? Nanny always had an answer.

Even after the fever had subsided, she remained out of sorts. Withdrawn and aloof, she sat on her bed, at times overwhelmed by a longing for her mother to be by her side. But her mother was engrossed in her own chores and had no spare time.

One day Kamal came and sat down next to her on her bed. "Tomorrow is the day of the fair," he whispered, but Munni remained her sullen self and ignored him.

"I could have taken you along to see the fair . . ." sighed Kamal, twitching his long upturned curly moustache, but Munni sat quite still, blinking her eyelids like someone drugged.

"You poor soul! Never ever been to a fair," sympathized Kamal.

"Oh yes I have! Didn't my father take me last year?" was the angry retort.

"That's no way to enjoy the fair – you weren't even allowed to get out of the carriage then."

The ice was breaking.

"There are such treats at the fair; the spectacle of a half-woman, half-vixen, the Ferris wheel, the snake and mongoose show, the toys." Kamal closed his eyes and counted off the attractions on his fingers one by one.

"We had a go on the Ferris wheel!" recalled Munni.

"What about the other attractions, the hot-spiced delicacies, the ice-cream, the fried goodies—"

Munni *Bibi* melted with delight. She had been on a bland diet for so long she could feel herself being tempted. The ice was broken and the strained relationship was mended once again.

The two of them reached such a secret understanding that even Munni's sisters could never have guessed how clever she, who kept gazing into space all day long, was being. A condescending smile played around her dried, parched lips as she beheld her sisters and their pathetic attempts to catch hold of the cat and marry it off to the doll.

All through the night Munni kept dreaming. Shops laden with toys, clay idols, rag-dolls and celluloid figures, dolls, doll-sized kitchen-ware, stoves, pots, pans and what not. Munni was no stranger to these attractions. They were brought to her house by the vending woman, but her mother always spoiled the fun. She boiled with rage at the sight of the woman's face, since she asked four *paise* for every toy and would still haggle over the price. Her mother bought the toys for her, but constantly grumbled at the waste of money, as they always fell to bits in no time at all. On getting a doll, Munni, bubbling with happiness, would run around all excited and fall over as a result; and the doll would inevitably shatter into a thousand fragments over the paved courtyard. Her joy would be shattered with it. Munni was always tempted by the rag-dolls in their colourful dresses. She yearned for one of them, with its large, slanted, kohl-laden eyes, but her mother never had either the time to make one or the inclination to buy one for her.

But her mother had no control over her dreams. She dreamed about owning all the dolls in the shop, and all the ice-creams and spiced delicacies which she lapped up in delight, uncaring of the germs. She also dreamed of her father's carriage with its white, frothy, flaming horse bringing her sisters to the fair in all their pomp and glory. Waking up in the dazzling morning, Munni found it hard to grasp that she had only been dreaming all night.

Rising with dignity, caring little for the ordinary mundane interests of the other children, she carried herself like a queen. She glanced at her sisters sitting around the ugly breakfast table, gobbling their breakfast of milk and bread. Munni was always irritated by the drab, unappetizing sight of breakfast and envied her parents, who were served tea – the fragrant golden liquid – in style, along with fried eggs and other treats. Although her brother was usually permitted these refreshments, the tea and eggs were a total taboo to the girls. It was only in winter that their bowls of milk were laced with tea. Their aunt had convinced their mother that eggs generated too much heat in the body and accelerated the growing process. Munni found that puzzling because whenever she touched an egg she found it cool. In any case, Munni *Bibi* never cared about the eggs. The half-cooked, jellyish fried eggs that they were given always looked so revolting.

"Let me see your face. Have you washed it properly?" one of the sisters asked, in the hope of finding some fault with her.

"Yes and I dried it too!" quipped Munni.

"Oh, you only pretended to wash, I can tell. But why not come and join us?"

Munni wanted to say that she had no desire to eat this homely food, as she had other treats in store, but Kamal had strictly forbidden her to talk about the fair in case the others pestered them to be taken too.

Since the tutor was on leave, as soon as breakfast was over the sisters ran off to spend the whole day playing in the backyard. Munni *Bibi* smiled as her sisters got out of her way. She knew that Kamal was waiting for her. First he was going to herd the other children off to the house of some relative, who found them a welcome sight, as she had no children of her own. She always made them each a paper flower and invariably treated them to sweets.

Engrossed in her fantasy, Munni finished the milk and was now waiting for the clatter of hooves and the sound of wheels starting off. She heard her father call farewell and the fading sound of the carriage, and heaved a sigh of relief.

Kamal came inside, flushed with pleasure, and dressed up to the hilt. He had tied a red scarf round his neck and had wound a ceremonial turban gallantly round his head.

"Look, Madam, even if Sahib hits me, he will not be able to tweak my ears as they are hidden in the folds of the turban."

"You really are a rascal! Be home before sunset or you'll be thrashed," her mother replied, trying not to laugh.

"I don't care about the fair. I am only trying to amuse the little sick child."

Kamal made it seem as if he was doing her mother a favour. He had Munni dressed in a red frock and pyjamas which were now a little tight. Munni, over-excited, was simply oblivious to the minor discomfort of pulling the narrow pyiamas over her heels. Yet when the nanny admonished Kamal for being unfair to the other children, Munni was surprised to find a soft spot in her heart for her sisters.

Kamal took out a cap all bedecked with sequins and with a crown of coloured feathers and placed it on Munni's head. This was the cap which Kamal had bought out of his own money for

Munni's birthday but which her mother had refused to let her wear. Instead, she had made him put it back in his box for his own future children when he got them.

There was a delicious warmth in the slanting sun-rays. Perched on Kamal's shoulders, the little maid looked around contentedly. The sparrows, spreading out their wings against the azure sky, flew down from the trees making small circles and landed on the ground, which they pecked with their little beaks before taking off into the air again. The nails on Kamal's shoes rang out on the coarse, uneven, stone-paved track. With her eyes shut Munni could have imagined herself riding a horse. But how could Munni shut her eyes when there was so much to see! She opened them wider and wider in the glare of the sun to drink in the approaching caravans of fun and laughter.

The buzz of the fair sounded like the humming of honey-bees. The postman came towards them carrying the day's post. He recognized the child in her fine attire.

"Where are you off to?"

"To the fair," pouted Munni as though she was being forced to go to her relations against her will. Actually at that moment she was thinking of her sisters who were not around to see her in all her glory.

The buzzing sound grew louder and louder. Rattling carts, packed to capacity with turban-clad men and colourfully dressed women, passed them by. The bullocks, straining under the load of carts weighed down with women and children, crawled slowly by. The atmosphere resounded with their excited, happy singing which seemed to keep time with the squeaking of the bullock cart. Munni was tired of sitting on Kamal's shoulder now and wanted him to hurry up, but he seemed to be living in a world of his own. The fair was at its peak. The squeaking of the Ferris wheel, the excited cries of women and children, the red and yellow *dupattas* fluttering on the Ferris wheel like flags, made a colourful sight. Amidst the general cheer and laughter Munni saw a huge, black image of *Rawan* made out of cardboard and paper. The toy stands and food-stalls seemed to have been sunk deep in a swirling flood of people.

The crowds of people made Munni imagine that the toys in the vendor's basket had come alive. The snake-charmer was playing his flute. A man who had painted himself with gaudy colours was inviting people to step inside the pitched tent and look at the spectacle of half-woman half-vixen. Munni wanted to stop at every stall to savour the delights but Kamal had forgotten all his promises. Cutting across the crowd, he was intent on going his own way. Sheer anger constricted her throat and two tear-drops settled in her eyes. When she turned round to look at the entertainment left behind, everything looked blurred because of the mist in her eyes. Placing her chin on top of Kamal's turban she peered down at Kamal's face, but the only thing she could see was the bushy, stiff moustache, which reminded her of the *Rawan* they had just seen.

At last Kamal stopped. Munni saw an old dilapidated door and the mud wall of a cottage.

"Are you hungry, Munni *Bibi?*" Kamal asked as he set her down on the ground. She shook her head vehemently in the hope that Kamal would notice her anger but he ignored it. When the door was unlatched, they found themselves inside a courtyard lined with cow-dung cakes. Although outside the fair was at its loudest, in here all that could be heard was the cluck, cluck of the black hen, feeding her chicks beside her pen. The goat tethered nearby was nibbling at hay and breathing out so hard that stalks flew about around it. The woman who unlatched the door looked down at the little girl, laughed aloud at her enraged expression and picked her up.

"I thought you were lying. I couldn't believe you'd bring the little girl here!"

She held her as though she was a priceless treasure, a basket full of delicacies. The little girl burst into tears at this display of affection. The pain of being carried away unceremoniously from the fair was simply too much! The woman stood still for a moment.

"Whatever are you crying for?" She asked in concern.

"Crying to see the fair," Kamal growled and irritably picked her up again. Before the child had time to burst into another fit of crying at Kamal's indifferent tone, the woman came to her rescue, admonishing Kamal, "Why didn't you take her to the fair first?"

"I thought you'd give her something nice to eat," laughed Kamal and held on to her *dupatta*. Jingling her anklet-bells, she pulled herself free from his grasp and ran to the pen, to catch a chick. The crying stopped the instant the little girl was clutching the snow-white chick in her hands. Standing beside the mud wall stacked with dung-cakes, Munni looked at the woman who was now giving water to the goat. She was dressed like her nanny at home, barefoot with jingling ankle-bells, bangle-covered arms, the bright nose-pin highlighting the kohl-filled eyes.

Carrying the live little ball of cotton-wool in her frock, she looked up at the woman's face, trying to recall where she'd seen her before. When the woman picked her up again her fragrance smelt familiar. It reminded her of her mother at home, who never had the time to pick her up and hold her close. In a little while the three of them were sitting all together on the bed like members of a close-knit family.

Munni *Bibi* looked around the homely dwelling, noticing the pots and pans neatly stacked on the stove and was amused by the tricks of the parrot in the cage hung nearby, pecking at bits of fruit. The woman showered affection on the little girl. Puffed up with her own importance, the little girl forgot all about the fair. But once she had exhausted all the amusements that the house offered, Munni *Bibi* once more recalled Kamal's promise. She wanted a doll and kicked up such a fuss that the woman rushed inside, and pulling down a bundle of old rags started work on a doll – the little girl held on to her *dupatta*.

A pillow was ripped open and its rag stuffing used for the doll. In the meantime the child felt drowsy. In her half-awake state, she saw Kamal tugging at the woman's sleeves.

"Aren't you ashamed of yourself!" She was angry and Kamal grunted disdainfully. Shaking her head to make herself stay awake, Munni was surprised to see tears in the woman's eyes. At that moment she hated the look on Kamal's face. Disgusted, she buried her face in the woman's lap and drifted into a deep sleep. When she woke up, the woman presented her with a beautifully made doll, with a mother-like bosom, its clothing bedecked all over with tinsel.

Kamal had gone. The fair was in full swing but Munni did not think of either of them. Holding on to the woman's dress, Munni followed her all around the house as she swept the floors clean, collected the refuse, caged up the hen and fed the parrot. After finishing her chores she washed the little girl, oiled her hair and lined her eyes with kohl and put a *bindya* on her forehead to ward off the "evil eye". Then she sat down to tidy herself and comb her hair.

"Did you get some jewels for the doll?" she asked Kamal as he entered the courtyard. She looked at him coolly.

Kamal threw the cheap jewellery in front of the woman and grasped the little girl by the hand.

"Let's go back, it's getting late!" But the little girl didn't want to go. "Hang on! The doll's not quite ready." The woman sounded hurt as she hastily stitched the jewellery on the rag-doll.

"I'll get you a doll from the fair," Kamal shouted and made for the door.

"You come with us too," pleaded the little girl. The woman handed over the finished doll and looked on helplessly.

Kamal stooped down to pick up the little girl but panicked when he caught sight of her kohl-lined eyes. He tried to rub it off with his handkerchief, then angrily walked off. Munni was surprised to see the woman running after them. She hurled a rupee at Kamal, telling him to take his money back, and then rushed back inside. Munni turned her head to watch and felt her heart tugged towards the woman, experiencing a strange pang of loneliness. Even Kamal now seemed a stranger.

He took her round the fair, treated her to all the promised delights and delicacies, showed her the toy shop; yet Munni remained cool and detached. All her excitement had subsided. She had simply lost all interest in the fair. He bought her a kohl-box but told her not to say a word about the kohl on her eyes or the doll in her hands. Munni took in little, being so distracted.

But her attention was caught and held by one particular woman in the fair, surrounded by a crowd of people, a drum beater, a harmonium player and a torch-bearer who kept close behind her. The woman was arranging her *dupatta* in the light of the torch; the *dupatta* was decorated with tinsel on one side only – why not on both sides Munni wondered – and then a flash of recognition shot up and down her whole being – the woman had danced outside her doorstep on the night Munni had given her the coins when everyone had said that she had committed a sin.

Terrified, she tugged at Kamal and tried to engage his attention but Kamal was hurriedly striding out of the fair. On the way Kamal told her to keep their rendezvous a secret but Munni was engrossed in a world of her own. It seemed as though she had left a part of herself somewhere in the fair. She thought of that white chick and the woman who had been – if only for a day – completely under her sway.

On reaching home, Kamal was immediately taken to task by Munni's father.

"Where on earth have you been?"

"To the fair."

"You lying scoundrel, I saw you stepping out of that whore's house!" growled the raging father, beginning to beat Kamal to a pulp.

Frightened out of her wits, the little girl cowered at her mother's side. She was filled with a contemptuous pity for Kamal. "He's gone and bought you this rubbish again, this filthy doll stuffed with dirty rags!" It was the mother's turn now. She shouted on and on and Munni *Bibi* longed to be out of her sight, high up in heaven with her doll.

Her mother now took a closer look at the doll and, smiling at her daughter, coaxed her to tell the truth. Munni soon came out with it, hoping that she would be rewarded by being allowed to keep the doll. But her mother looked at the doll's full bosom and, shaking her head in disapproval, cursed the "bad" women who corrupted children with their cheap tricks.

The nanny snatched up the doll and threw it straight into the stove. This so terrified Munni she thought she would be the next thing to be tossed into the fiery furnace. She burst out crying, and her loud wails brought her father once again storming out of his room, whereupon he set upon Kamal, showering him with resounding slaps.

Originally translated from the Urdu
by Iffat Saeed

The Poison of Loneliness

Musarrat Kalanchvi

He moved slowly towards the bear. Its hair was erect like a hedgehog's. It was standing with its paws raised and its red tongue visible inside its open mouth. The bear looked bloodthirsty, with burning eyes – eyes that could set everything on fire.

Jugnoo, on the other side, felt the same way, as if the blazing sun was within himself. His veins were burning and his whole body felt a crushing pain. He advanced with open hands, pounced upon the bear and smashed it. The tiny toy bear could not take such a torrent of anger. Jugnoo's passion was pacified and he felt a slight chill descend over him.

It seemed as if the bear was once again assuming its old form and its soul was returning to its body. This time the bear started chasing him as if to take revenge. Jugnoo retreated and clung to the wall of his room. He often did this and ran towards his nanny, Sakina, to hide in her lap.

His mother left early in the morning for work and came back in the evening. Sakina later went to the servants' quarters to feed her daughter and if Jugnoo demanded anything, she would often ignore him or tell him off. There was a wall between her room and Jugnoo's. Jugnoo looked at the wall with his head raised. There he could see a picture of a kangaroo with a baby kangaroo in its pouch. The little kangaroo was sitting with its tiny tongue sticking out and one little hand in the air.

Jugnoo felt as if the young kangaroo was making faces at him and teasing him with its gestures. Once again he grew aggressive and tried to climb up the wall and tear off the picture. But alas, the picture was out of his reach just as his own mother was. He tried to climb on the table to reach it but lost his balance and fell down.

He started crying bitterly. Sakina appeared from the other room, picked him up in her arms, gave him biscuits and played with him, but nothing could stop him crying. Jugnoo had been hurt somewhere deep inside and his sobs turned into loud cries.

Finally Sakina left him on his own. He lay on the floor and when he raised his head, his face was wet and the cheeks were pale with moisture glistening on them.

Jugnoo went to find Sakina but she was not in her room. Then he went out on to the verandah but Sakina was nowhere to be seen. All of a sudden, a strange fear seized him . . . he was terribly afraid of being left alone by everyone. How alone he felt at that moment!

He knew that he was searching for something. His feelings were innocent and his sentiments pure. He had a simple heart full of longing. In spite of so many possessions he was marooned by a sense of deprivation. A moment of sadness engulfed his whole being. Immersed in a sea of loneliness he felt himself drowning. Something was choking him; he could not comprehend this feeling. He could not resist letting out a loud cry and this cry shook everything around him. He felt as if his blazing tears and sighs were burning everything . . . the roof, the walls and the floor. His pale face reflected the way he was feeling and he came indoors once again.

There were two plants in the corner, a pitcher was near the water tap and a chair stood beside the table. A ball and hockey stick were also placed next to each other. All these looked very fine but Jugnoo was standing there all alone. He felt like a stranger there.

He started thinking; perhaps one of the jasmine plants was the mother of the other plants. The tap and the pitcher, the table and the chair, the hockey stick and the ball; everything had a mother. Why was he without a mother? Where was she? No, there was no mother here. Mothers went to work and all Sakinas simply went to their homes after beating "Jugnoos". Then who could be the playmate of children? Who could mother them? Why were things together while Jugnoo was all alone?

Little Jugnoo was at a loss to fathom out all this muddle; he clenched his fists and once again his cry was absorbed by the vibrating air. His own sobs whispered in his ears and he could hear the throbbing of his tiny heart.

His sense of loneliness suffocated him as if someone was trying to kill him; as if caught up in a cloud of smoke he was begging for a puff of air in order to breathe.

His fear was so overpowering he felt like hiding himself in some place where nothing could frighten him. But where to go? At that moment, he caught sight of the stairs that went up to the roof. A railing ran up both sides. To Jugnoo those railings looked like arms ready to embrace him. He climbed up and went out on to the roof.

Out there everything looked fresh. There was a feeling of openness around him. A cool breeze was blowing. When this air rustled through his hair, a feeling of joy soaked his whole being and for a moment there was peace all around him. Air started brushing through his hair and its swiftness lulled him, soothing his senses. He wondered if the air was his mother. But why was it invisible? Jugnoo started calling his mother, "Mama, come on, come to me, I am afraid, I want to see you."

His warm cries could not rouse any feelings from the cold air. Once again he felt sad and his eyes came winding back through the maze of this sadness. As his eyes came to rest upon the roof floor, he saw a shadow. It was his own shadow and was bigger than him. He noticed that wherever he went, his shadow always led him.

Then it dawned upon him that now he was no longer alone, his own self was with him, was visible to him. It might even be looking at him. He felt like catching it so that it could not slip away, could not go to work like his mother.

He stepped forward to snatch at the shadow but he managed to catch nothing but the emptiness of his own hand. Jugnoo grew angry once again and shouted in the air, "Mama, if you don't come to me, I will also leave you."

He drew himself in to show his displeasure and took a step back. He sensed that someone was chasing him, perhaps to make friends.

On turning round, he saw that once again, it was nothing but his own shadow. When Jugnoo stopped, it also stood still.

He started enjoying this chase; at times he felt pleased and at times he felt angry. His shadow kept with him wherever he went. He started playing tricks; he would tease it by going this way and that, but his shadow always stuck close to him.

Jugnoo liked this game of hide-and-seek and moved towards the railing round the roof. There was a huge tree growing close by, spreading cool and comforting shade across the floor of the roof. But as Jugnoo stepped into this shade his own shadow disappeared. Once again he felt afraid. His heart began to beat faster and he shrieked plaintively.

Then he noticed the chimney on the roof.

He went over, and there he discovered a sparrow's nest built inside the chimney. A little baby sparrow sat in it, chirping. Jugnoo was so happy to see another young creature like himself. He saw himself in that bird and exclaimed sadly that it was lonely and sad, just like him.

He decided to make it his playmate. He pictured how loving they would be with each other, living and playing together and sharing their loneliness. Neither of them would ever leave this place and they would always look after each other.

His heart was throbbing with joy as he stretched out his hand towards the young sparrow. But at that very moment, he felt a sharp bite. Who could have known that a snake was hidden nearby!

Jugnoo raised a great scream – his very last.

Nobody gave a thought to the fate of the young sparrow – whether perhaps it too had been bitten by the very same snake.

Originally translated from the Seraiki
by Rakhshanda Ashiq

The Coach
Nilofar Iqbal

The bicycle fell with a loud clang and hit the concrete floor of the courtyard. Guddoo was so scared that he stood leaning against the wall, stiff and unable to move. Because of the dread, his eyes popped out of their sockets, and he stood staring at the closed door of his father's bedroom. Exactly as he had feared, the door opened and his father, dour-looking, with bloodshot eyes, emerged from his room grumbling. First he bent down to examine the bicycle. The light had been smashed and the brand new paint had chipped off in a number of places. Unable to contain his anger, he began foaming at the mouth. "I'm going to kill you today, you little shit," he roared as he dragged Guddoo off by his skinny arm.

"Where's my cane?" he inquired. It was for such contingencies that a thin, pliable mulberry cane had been kept. It stood in one corner of the yard.

Guddoo's mother and the rest of his brothers and sisters stood by, silent, holding their breath. One tiny mistake, one wrong move by any of them could turn that cane in their direction, even though they were all agreed that Guddoo did deserve some punishment. That bicycle had been acquired after an eager, enthusiastic and long wait. The father had taken up the offer by his factory to purchase the bicycle in easy instalments. He had been exceptionally excited the day he brought the bicycle home. He had also brought home a bag of candies and a big watermelon. It was like the Eid celebration in the house. The father announced that he planned to get a colourful basket for the front of the bicycle as well as plastic flowers to decorate it. He said he would also install two side-view mirrors on it. Even the mother felt cheerful that day because the father was so happy; usually, when he came in from the factory at the end of the day, he was irritable from his long, tiring walk back home. One child or other always got a thrashing. The mother was of course used to being scolded. But Guddoo's crime today was too serious. The children all stood breathless, waiting to see what Guddoo would get.

The blows from the cane came raining down on Guddoo's emaciated body. Smarting with pain and screaming, he fell down on the floor and started begging his father to stop. He tried to hold off the blows with his hands.

"I'll skin you alive," screamed the father. He was livid. The mother could finally take it no longer and ran to the child's rescue, protecting him with her arms. The cane had left white marks on the child's clenched hands. She couldn't bear it: "Stop it now! Are you going to take his life for a little thing like that?"

"A little thing! That a little thing? He's ruined the new bicycle. You always spoil him. I'll put him straight in ten minutes. He's not going to get away with it today. I'm going to teach him a lesson." He pulled Guddoo away from his mother and dragged him to the coal-shed. It was where they stored coal, waste paper and rubbish. He pushed Guddoo in and bolted the door from outside. Throwing a threatening look at everyone, he waved the cane and said, "Nobody had better touch the bolt until I say so, or he'll be skinned alive too."

He examined the bicycle once again, rubbed his fingers on the places where the paint had chipped off, picked up the broken pieces of glass, glared at everybody with his bloodshot eyes and walked back into his room dragging his slippered feet.

Guddoo lay sobbing on the dusty floor of the coal-shed feeling sharp stabs of pain in his ribs and back. It was a very hot and sultry day in June. The tiny closet blazed like an oven. He felt terribly thirsty, and began to feel suffocated. He got up and started banging on the door with both hands, shouting, "Mother, mother, give me some water."

When no one came near the door, he sat down exhausted and breathless on the floor. The floor felt cool to the touch. He lay down with his cheek against it. Waste paper and sheets torn from magazines lay scattered about. Guddoo's uncle used to make money from recycling waste paper. Guddoo was suddenly attracted by a colourful picture on one page. He brought it up close to his eyes, and gazed at it attentively. It was the picture of a coach driven by six horses, racing along a flower-strewn track. At the far end of the track stood a golden palace; the coach seemed to be moving towards it. Its seats were upholstered in maroon velvet and decorated with tassels. The state of the shed forgotten, Guddoo was lost in the picture. Red plumes adorned the foreheads of the horses, which were proudly trotting along towards the palace. The most beautiful thing about the coach was its wheels – immense in size and golden. Guddoo lost himself in the beauty and glitter of the wheels.

And lo, the coach started moving. "I must run and catch it," Guddoo decided. He jumped into the coach, and soon sank into a cushiony, comfortable seat. As soon as he was inside the coach, he felt a cool breeze blowing. "This is wonderful," he thought. He was being bumped up and down with the thumping of the horses' hooves. Perhaps the coach would go into the park which he could see ahead. "There I'll surely be able to get some nice cold water." The track that the coach was running along was shaded by thick trees and the smell of new leaves hung in the air. Guddoo started taking in deep breaths.

The horses came to a stop in front of the park gates. Guddoo leapt out of the coach. He felt as light as a butterfly.

Bouncing up and down like a rubber ball, he skipped into the park. He had never seen a place like that before, not even in a dream. Like a small fairy he flitted about on the grass. He seemed to have forgotten his thirst. Then a rainbow-coloured butterfly caught his eye. He ran after it.

"Don't catch it. Its wings will break," he heard someone say in a gentle voice. He turned round and saw a woman, lovely as could be and dressed in the most beautiful gown. He had never before set eyes on anyone like her. Gently, lovingly, she pulled Guddoo towards her. Her clothes smelled nice too. Guddoo felt as though she was his mother. But no, how could that be? His mother's clothes always smelled of garlic and stale perspiration. Guddoo hid his face in the woman's bosom. His burning forehead found comfort in the coolness and fragrance of her gown.

"Come with me." Holding his hand, she moved towards the palace. Guddoo felt as if he had seen that palace somewhere before; everything seemed so familiar.

"That cupboard has sweet drinks in it," he told her, pointing with his finger. She laughed.

"Yes, it does, but how did you know?" she frowned, feigning surprise.

"I just did," Guddoo said proudly.

The woman took out a bottle of fruit drink from the cupboard and began filling him glass after glass of it.

"Enough, thank you, enough. If I don't stop now, my tummy will burst," Guddoo said, rubbing his hand over his stomach.

"You are a good boy," the woman said and, pushing his hair back, kissed him on the forehead.

"Come, let's play." Holding his hand she led him away. Guddoo noticed other children playing in the park as well. Colourful puffy clouds, green, pink, lilac and white, floated about. Guddoo was tempted to touch them, to run inside them. He ran after a green cloud. He stretched out his hand to touch it. Oh, it was like a snowball. A piece of the cloud came off in his hand! He tasted it. It was as sweet as candy-floss. He pulled off a really big piece and, sucking on it joyfully, turned back to the woman.

"A man sells candy-floss like this in our street, but it always leaves a bitter taste in my mouth at the end. This stuff is really sweet."

"Let's go to the canal." The woman took Guddoo by the hand and began to run. Guddoo laughed to see her run so fast, but he knew he could outrun her. So he ran past and left her far behind.

"I won, I won," he called, raising his arms as he got to the canal, way ahead of the woman. There were lots of other children bathing in the canal. The water came up to their waists. Guddoo jumped in with his clothes on. "Oh, this cold, cold water," he screamed with joy, swimming like a fish, sometimes diving in, sometimes splashing about. The woman, smiling, kept an eye on him from the bank.

After a while she said, "Come out now. It's getting late. Look, the coach has come to take you back."

Alarmed, he raised his head above the water and saw the coach standing nearby.

"No, I don't want to go back," he said with a fretful shake of his head, and, kicking his legs vigorously, swam far away in the water.

The woman laughed. "All right," she said. "As you wish. But you have to come out of the water now."

"No. First send the coach away."

The woman gestured to the coach. It began to move off and disappeared in a grove of trees far away.

The woman helped him out of the canal. "You're tired," she said. "Take a little nap. Let me help you go to sleep."

The two walked towards a shady tree and sat down on the cool grass under it. She placed his head in her lap and slowly began combing his hair with her fingers. Guddoo had an unbearable feeling of utter peace, and his eyes began to close. Gradually, he sank into deep sleep.

When Guddoo's father lifted him up from the dusty floor, his dust-covered cheeks were streaked with two white lines of tears.

"He's fallen asleep," he said, laying him down on the bed next to his mother. The boy's head drooped to one side.

The mother shook him, "He's not asleep, he's unconscious," she screamed, looking at her husband with eyes full of anger and contempt.

The father jumped on to the bicycle and, swearing at the extreme heat, began pedalling quickly down to the physician's nearby.

Originally translated from the Urdu
by Faruq Hassan

The Magic Flower

Parveen Malik

Sakina was born into an extremely poor family. Except for when they were asleep, her parents worked hard all day long. And even then, they couldn't afford two square meals a day. How much was a rural wage earner worth? These luckless people demanded little. They worked wherever they found a job, took such wages as were offered and thanked God for it.

It was time for the wheat harvest. This gave daily wage earners the chance not only to make money but also to gather up ears of wheat left behind by the harvesters and make a few *seers* of grain. The mother put the six-month-old Sakina in an open-ended knapsack tied to a *charpoy* under the shade of a tree. She also gave her a grain of opium to ensure the child would sleep. Satisfied that everything had been taken care of, she started off for the fields where she was to work. The owner of the farm had either sown an early variety of wheat or else had been careless, for stalks crackled at a touch of the hand and wheat fell in every direction.

Sakina's mother worked with the sickle at great speed, happy in the hope that the more she harvested, the larger her share of fallen grain would be. Working, she lost all sense of time. She had wanted to return home by midday but now the sun was sliding westward. Eventually, putting a big bag of the ears of grain on her head, she decided to go home. Much time had passed. The shade over Sakina had moved away long ago. Her eyes were all swollen with crying. When the mother lifted her to her bosom it was as though she had picked up a live coal. She took water from a pitcher lying close by and sprinkled it over Sakina's face so she was able to open her eyes but by evening her mouth was drawn to one side. Her mother beat her breasts raw and cried, "Oh, she is a girl, what will become of her now?" Sakina's parents went to the shrine of every holy man in the region. There were amulets of every hue on her shoulders and around her neck but Sakina's fate had been decided. The Moving Finger, having writ, had moved on.

With saliva constantly dribbling from her crooked mouth, Sakina continued to grow. As she grew bigger, so did her mother's worries. One day when Sakina was playing with other girls in the street, one of the girls kept on cheating at the game. Sakina tried, in her stuttering voice, to tell the girl to behave. The culprit, her eyes shining with mischief, said, "What does the crooked flute say?" This was a cue for the rest of the children. They made a circle around her and started to dance and sing, "Crooked flute, crooked flute!" Sakina tried for some time to hit at them but when she could not catch a single one, she went off to her mother, crying. The mother's eyes were already red from trying to set fire to damp dung-cakes. She was beside herself with rage when Sakina told her what had happened to her in the street. "The children are not wrong when they call you a crooked flute. Why do you mix with them? Why can't you stay indoors?" Sakina's mother spanked her and then made her sit by her side. Sakina now had nothing to do all day except tease the goat or strew the ash from the oven all over the place and get beaten again by her mother. For the next few weeks, Sakina's mother watched her daughter's behaviour and glowered. Then, one day, she washed Sakina's saliva-dribbling face, combed her hair, gave her a freshly washed dress and took her to a teacher. "Look after this scamp, please; perhaps then someone might one day ask for her hand. Otherwise, she'll remain the fool she is."

And so Sakina was admitted to school. She was determined, it appeared, to get even with the girls who called her a crooked flute. She soon knew every lesson by heart. She could always answer every question put by the teacher and would raise her arm impatiently as if flying a flag of victory.

One day, the teacher was in a black mood and kept telling the girls off. Suddenly she caught sight of Sakina's dark arm raised. From the arm her eyes dropped to her face and she felt sickened. "Get up, Sakina, and sit at the back," she said harshly. But Sakina had by now become quite adept at reading people's eyes. With her head lowered, she got up silently and sat down behind the rest of the girls. Her hand fell into her lap like the dead branch of a tree, never again to turn green.

Close to the school was a graveyard. Between earthen and cemented graves, there were a lot of berry-bearing trees whose fruit was quite sweet. During the break, school girls would go to the graveyard and romp around. One day one of the girls let her foot fall on the family grave of Malik Nadir Khan. A peasant employed by Malik Akbar Khan happened to see this and gave an exaggerated account of it to his landlord. The Malik sent a message to the school-teacher, asking her to stop her students from going to the graveyard or else he would have the school closed down. The worried teacher ordered the school helper, Mai Nekan, to somehow stop the girls. Mai Nekan went up to the school, grumbling all the while. "How can I stop them? These girls are like young cattle," she said to herself. But something had to be done, and at last she thought of a way out. During the break she would gather the girls around her and tell them stories about countries where princesses as beautiful as the moon and princes as bright as the sun lived.

The girls soon got bored with these stories and invented new ways of enjoying themselves within the school compound, but

Sakina latched herself on to Mai Nekan. She would find herself in far-off countries and get lost in the magic of the school helper's stories for hours on end. She couldn't understand how people in those countries were always happy and when she could contain herself no longer, she would ask Mai Nekan for an answer. Her questions made life difficult for Mai Nekan. Once she asked the Mai, "Auntie, if someone gets hold of the magic flower, are all her problems solved? Can she also transform her face?" The Mai replied coldly, "You stupid girl, why should we bother with faces. Just let our two hands be safe, that's enough for us." Sakina fell silent but deep inside her, questions were weaving themselves like a ball of silken thread.

One winter night, strange sounds were heard coming from the graveyard as if a thousand evil spirits were yelling in unison. People came out of their homes, alarmed. "What's happened?" everyone asked everyone else. But no one had the courage to go into the graveyard to see what was going on. At last, Aslam Khan, cursing all and sundry, dared two of his sturdily built servants to go in and find out. They proceeded gingerly with lanterns in their hands. And then everyone saw her – bare-headed, with her hair dishevelled, oblivious to her torn dress: Sakina was shrieking like a mad thing, with saliva drooling all the way down to the hem of her shirt. "Whatever has happened to you?" Aslam Khan asked her sternly. She managed to stop the shrieking but her mouth stayed wide open. Soft sobs shook her whole frame.

"Why won't you tell me what's happened?" Aslam Khan asked even more sternly.

She replied in a trembling voice, "He told me that if I came to the graveyard, he would give me the magic flower but . . ." She began to shake as if caught in a storm. There was utter silence for a long time. It was broken by a woman who said, "The filthy beasts – even her they didn't spare." Another woman said softly, "Well, you can't see faces in the dark, can you, sister."

And then they all went back to their homes, smiling amongst themselves, because not one of them had need of the magic flower.

Originally translated from the Punjabi
by Zafar Iqbal Mirza

Farewell to the Bride

Khadija Mastoor

A very thin trickle of water was crawling along the narrow drain, with foamy soap-suds enveloping it almost like a protective cover. He had just emerged from the dark bathroom after taking a bath and, while drying his hair with a towel, dragged an easy chair out to the courtyard to sit in the sun, to warm up his stiff, cold body. His glance fell on the drain as he rubbed his hair with the towel. Water was flowing through in stops and starts, and suddenly he recalled the incident that had so strangely affected his over-sensitive heart and soul. For several days after it had happened he had been unable to think of anything else, but then slowly, with time, he had begun to forget it had ever taken place. But now, after so many days, that thin trickle of water with its soap-suds had once again reminded him of that fateful day. From the depths of his heart he could hear sighs of pain; his pain. Once again he began to relive the emotions and sensations he had felt that fateful day. Although before that morning he had seen and experienced many events that could melt even a heart of stone, he had never been so deeply affected as this.

The hustle and bustle of the city had been lost in the echoes of death. Living beings were hiding in nooks and crannies, crying for solace. Desolation was everywhere and it almost seemed as if death was stalking anyone and anything alive, lying in wait to pounce and devour it. But the sensitive hearts of the social work committee members refused to accept that life was so cheap or that human beings should be ignored like insects attempting to crawl out of this web of death. So, wherever they could reach, they sought out people crying without hope, transferring them to the safety of relief camps. That entire day he had spent combing the deserted city from corner to corner searching for victims of the riot and transporting them to the camp sites. Exhausted and bone-weary, he had been walking home from the police station. It was about five o'clock in the evening and he had been in a hurry to get home for a well-earned rest when suddenly he stopped. Just ahead of him about a dozen men were bending over, peering closely at something of interest coming out of an open drain. He went closer and saw that the main entrance door of the house had a huge lock on the outside which the group was contemplating breaking open.

"Three days ago we got rid of every single occupant of this house including the children, yet how come this fellow escaped us?" said a man with bloodshot eyes and a terrifying face, waving his knife.

"Then break the lock, man," said another, extricating his foot from his dangling *kamarband*. "But how come there's a lock on the door? How can anyone still be inside?" he said, trying to fathom it out.

"If no one's there, could there be magic at work?" remarked the third one, gesticulating wildly and pointing at the drain, rolling his red eyes. Running through the drain of the building was soapy water, plain for all to see.

"I reckon some kind of bath ritual's being performed," said a fourth man, cleaning up his knife on his shirt.

For a moment he thought of dashing back to the police station for help but it was too far away and there was no policeman in sight.

"Break the lock!" growled the mob.

"Look, in the name of humanity . . . " He was trying to calm the group down and reason with them, but his argument was cut short.

"When our mothers, sisters and brothers were being butchered and bathed in blood, where was your humanity then? Where were you?" many voices asked together.

"Sleeping with his humanity, no doubt," the one with bloodshot eyes and a terrifying face cackled demonically.

"Now, look here . . ." He tried again but dropped his hands in despair.

"The lock's going to be broken. Why do you want to stop us?" And the whole group began to look at him as if he were an outsider, not one of them.

"I am not stopping you. Go ahead, break the lock," he said in desperation, knowing full well that at that moment no one would listen to him anyway, whether he opposed or contradicted them or not. They were fully capable of tearing him limb from limb.

The lock broke open easily and within a few moments the whole group stormed into the house. He was the last to walk in, trying to keep a grip on his anxiety as his mind raced around in circles. If only he could conjure up some way to save the fugitive clearly hiding somewhere in the house. Suddenly he hit upon a weak but possible plan of action.

"Listen," he cautioned the group. "Don't walk about so casually; maybe he has a gun. I have a rifle, so let me go ahead. You follow behind, but keep quiet," he said almost in a whisper. They all agreed and began to follow him. He started up the stairs, slowly, one at a time so the staircase became a never-ending climb. A whole day's running around had left him physically and mentally exhausted, yet at that moment he did not feel the least bit tired. As he climbed on, he recalled that this tall building had been one of the first to be attacked and not one soul had been left here alive. How come then this person had managed to escape?

His plan was to signal quietly to the fugitive as soon as he saw him, that he should hide himself and save his life. "I'll warn him that his death is following close on my heels." He was confident that the fugitive would know of some other hide-out within the house.

They went up past the first storey, then the second, then the third. At each level, the group searched every corner thoroughly but failed to find anyone. He would be the first to enter each room, but each time he was met with silence and emptiness, almost as if the place was haunted. He had witnessed some horrible barbaric scenes of human massacre and knew he did not have the strength to witness yet another such event. His pace increased. He left the group way behind. Reaching the top of the last staircase, he entered the room ahead and froze. A beautiful, tall girl in clean, blue clothing was sitting on the floor. Her nose was red and her eyes swollen from crying. She looked tired, utterly exhausted and drained. Her long flowing hair was loose and she was combing it. Beside her on the floor was the damning evidence of a soap-dish, a towel, a clip and some hairpins. He could not believe his eyes. Was she a fairy or a spirit? She was too beautiful to be real! The girl raised her heavy eyes and saw him standing there and the comb slipped from her hands. He wanted to save this lovely apparition. His whole soul cried out for him to somehow protect her. He gesticulated to her to hide and told her in hushed tones that other people were following him. But the girl sat as if turned to stone. She did not move, but looked at him in desperation and then bowed her head. Soon the crowd was inside the room, waving their knives and grinning devilishly.

"We dug a mountain and only found a mouse," said the man with the bloodshot eyes, stepping forward. The girl's face turned ashen.

"Have pity, don't touch her, don't touch her," he shouted wildly, placing himself between the assailant and the girl.

"Why shouldn't we touch her? Afraid her body'll get spoiled? Get out of the way, young man!" said someone and they all started to laugh as two men shoved him away from the girl.

"No! No!" He screamed and attempted again to place himself in front of the girl but the red-eyed man laid his knife at his chest in warning. Then he picked up the girl and slung her over his shoulders like a sacrificial animal. The girl did not utter a sound. She offered no resistance at all but as they were taking her off, she spread her dangling arms open towards him, silently begging for help. He wished at that moment that the knife had entered his heart. He advanced towards the girl but they shoved him back again and the man with the bloodshot eyes yanked the girl's arms up around his own neck. She closed her eyes as if in great pain.

Suddenly the room was empty and even more quiet than before. They had all gone and he found himself sitting in the same place on the floor where just a few moments earlier the girl had been sitting, combing her long hair. He had failed to save her and that thought made him burst out crying like a baby. Some indescribable emotion was making him weep. He had seen dozens of young women abducted, heard their protests and their cries and his heart had always somehow remained unmoved. But this girl's silent appeal for help had touched his very soul in a manner he found too painful to admit.

Having exhausted his emotions with crying, he picked up her pins and hair-clip that had been trodden on so callously and held them in his hands. He touched them gently and stroked the still damp towel. Then he glanced at the bed which still had wrinkles on its covers as if some restless soul had tossed and turned on it anxiously throughout the night. He began to think once again about that strange girl and how she must have passed those three days and three nights here. He got up and straightened the covers of the bed. The pillow was stained with her tears. She must have cried non-stop for three days and three nights and then probably had got up exhausted and washed her face to muster strength only to cry yet again. Then she must have begun to comb her hair. But why was she combing her hair, why had she washed her face with soap? She could easily have just wiped her face with a wet towel or sprinkled it with water. But she was getting ready. For what or for whom?

The city was silent. The building too was deathly silent. There was no living soul nearby and yet she was getting ready, adorning herself, even though she had been alone in a room for three days. What had moved her to do that? Why? All these unanswered questions crowded his brain.

And then, when they had picked her up, she had gone with them without a murmur. His heart and soul went out to her as he thought of her again. If only he could hold that tired girl and lay her head on his shoulder and rest her swollen eyelids. He picked up the pillow from the bed and placed it on his lap. A crumpled piece of paper had been lying under it. It was old and dirty. He opened it and began to read. "My darling. I will soon be coming to meet you. I am so desperate to see you again. Even if there's a catastrophe, it will not stop me reaching you. I will come directly to your room, where you will be waiting for me, all dressed up and . . ." The letter fluttered from his hand and drifted to the floor.

Suddenly there was a commotion downstairs. He could hear loud noises, thumps and bangs. Maybe a neighbouring building was being looted. He put the hair-clips and pins in his pocket and with faltering steps descended the stairs and silently walked home.

He looked at the open drain again. The water had stopped flowing and the soapy foam had subsided.

Originally translated from the Urdu
by Moneeza Hashmi

The Cow

Firdous Haider

Startled, she lifted her henna-painted hands and breathed in the fragrance of the jasmine bracelets knotted at her wrists. As she touched the tinsel in her hair-parting, the scent of the flowers and the flame-coloured henna aroused in her an anxious longing.

The henna wished to sparkle, the tinsel wanted to be kissed and the half-open buds of her lips longed to blossom into flowers. But all was still.

Things resembled a hot, humid night when leaves hold their breath, the whispering wind becomes silent and time stands still, masking all with anguish. That night was also such a night . . . a night that was long awaited. Her fragrance-drenched body was like a mine, awaiting a footstep.

Moment by moment, time went by; one moment spread over aeons and then aeons passed by. She kept on waiting. But everything was still; loneliness and restlessness persisted.

The bellowing of the cow, like the sound of a stone falling into a deep well, created commotion in the quiet alley, as if it too was weary of bearing the grief of the desolate monotony of immobile moments, and now, breaking loose, it was off in search of a companion . . . its longing was now intense.

People, peeping from their windows and doors, with dazed, tired and discontented faces, just watched the cow, but young, unmarried girls and women, suffering the agony of separation from their spouses, knew that it had broken loose because it wanted to conceive – and envy sparkled like glow-worms in their eyes. They knew that this was its right and that exploitation of the animal ended only when it mustered enough strength to break away. It drew this strength only from an instinctive passion to create.

That night was the mother of all nights – it was a night that longed to surrender. When it stood still, not moving, she lifted her eyes.

He was there.

With all his existence, with all her faith he was there. But he wasn't there. She lowered her eyes again. She had accepted what she did not know. She had had no say in it. Others had selected him for her but she wanted to own him, confess faith in him, adore him, worship him. The mother of nights was killed. Moments that were to be created in its womb were crucified.

He was there but without the ability to create. He, who was there, insisted on being acclaimed god. He wanted authentication of what he did not possess.

"You will love me, bow down before me, worship me, for I am your god. You will get food and shelter in this house and protection from the intensity of changing seasons; so eat, drink and bellow, but stay tied to your peg."

Thus she was commanded.

She kept listening and musing on how she should accept and obey. She could not bow down in return for food. Devotion emanates in the form of light rays from the inner self. But here everything was empty and desolate, from the innermost to the outermost, and her heart was not inclined to stoop.

Devotion in return for shelter and protection – this was unjust. Without probing or investigating she was tied up to a peg where all the amenities of life were available . . . all except what instinct desired, what nature craved for.

That longing, *that* love and *that* vigour which could sanctify creation and give her the status of motherhood, fill her bosom with motherly feelings and make her sway on the earth like a fruit-laden tree.

Her eyes blindfolded with a golden veil and her feet enchained with crimson, tinkling chains, she was forced to bow down.

When that night, which was the mother of all nights and after . . . all other nights remained silent, the woman inside her opened out like a shell. When no drop of pearl entered the shell, that woman wept and frustration engulfed her whole being.

He who was chosen to be her god – he himself was aware of his inadequacy, but with his stronger physique tried to hide his weakness. That is why he wished her to stoop, was unjust, cruel and selfish. He wanted to prove himself superior.

She tried to worship him but could not. She stayed tied to the peg. Her body smouldered. She was compelled to lay aside her conscience but her passion kept stirring and her insight grew deeper, sharper.

It was then that the anguish of her soul heard a voice, a voice that drowned out all other voices, which was bearing the drop towards the ocean, the part towards the whole. She grew more restless. Like the flute, she tried to find solace in the rhythm of her grief. She was now convinced that when her grief reached its peak, the awaited moment would arrive, and it was this faith that kept the flame of hope alive.

People said it was nerves. This grief, this waiting, this faith. But she kept developing unconquerable power. Fearing her, the god tightened his grip and with the aid of scientific men kept pouring sleeping potions down her throat. He was in no way prepared to let the cow go free. She was the symbol of his manliness, the seal of its confirmation.

Love can split a mountain, iron can break iron but there is no device to crush the desire to create.

And then . . .

In a state of trance she felt no hut was too small and no palace large enough; no diamond precious and no stone worthless. She realized that the ruler had become the ruled, the master had become the slave. She saw a mountain like the Sinai, heard a voice like the Scripture and discerned a light that was Knowledge.

Then came the revelation for the *drop*.

A drop which is greater than oceans, which is a pearl inside the shell, which is priceless, which is the earth, the time, the omnipresent.

The rhythm of the flute grew faster; it mingled with passion; the sky and the earth united and she knew that the moment had arrived. That awaited moment. She ripped the golden veil and broke open the iron chains.

People wanted to snatch that moment from her, for they did not know of that pain – the pain which is also the fountain of fulfilment, which leads to the abandonment of worldly riches.

Sadists wanted to stone her to death. But now the chains were broken and she was advancing to her destination. She kept on walking and running and she was continually chased.

Now she was transformed into an energy that wanted to interact with another force and begin the process of creation. And this was but natural; it was bound to happen. The moment in which the process of creation begins is the mother of moments. Its denial is impossible and its acceptance inevitable. Its confirmation does not require proclamation.

Those who were chasing her with stones in their hands reached the place where she stood with ineluctable decision. They saw the light emanating from her being and they saw her bow down before a power that protected her, dominated her, whose superiority she accepted. They saw a haven of light under which she flowed like liquid silver.

A liquid – which at times took the colour of henna, at times transformed the buds of the lips into blossoms and at times became the fragrance of flower-bracelets.

Now lips were lips no more, henna was no longer henna and bracelets were no longer bracelets. All mingled in unison. She was no longer afraid of anyone. She was not afraid of those with stones in their hands.

Then, when all the weary and frustrated sat oblivious behind half-open windows and doors, the cow which had broken loose returned.

And on her return she announced that she had conceived life.

Originally translated from the Urdu
by Yasmin Hameed

The Valley of Doom

Noor-ul-Huda Shah

All roads lead to death. And life is walking barefoot along them. The dark, burning, coal-tar road, the flaming sky, the desolation . . . and the side-by-side, step-by-step, blistering journey of man and woman.

"Just look . . . no shelter on this promising earth . . . nowhere – and – and why are you staring at me like this! No, no, don't stare at me so wide-eyed – your death-like gaze frightens me . . ." She takes hold of his hand and comes to a halt but in response, the man's look turns colder – icier – more death-like.

The woman feels the river of death flowing into her sinews, her veins and every last drop of her blood. Her voice wobbles while speaking. "For centuries, I have dreamt of a small, peaceful home. Will it ever come true!" Her voice seems to die mid-sentence.

"Home!" His laughter has the bitterness of poison. "I wonder! Can any walls provide shelter? Is every home inhabited? So many are occupied by bestial humans and humanoid beasts! Is there any wall high enough to ward off death? Why don't you answer me now?" It is as if acrid smoke fills his eyes.

They both sit under a leafless tree whose bare branches have lost the strength to resist the heat of the sun. Exhausted, the man covers his eyes with his hand. Silence lies between them for long moments – and at the end of this stillness, she rests her lips on his hand and whispers.

"Do you realize . . . that . . . that . . . I'm going to have a baby!"

He takes his hand from his face and his eyes lock with those of the woman.

"No!" He barely manages to say.

"Why! Didn't you marry me? Wasn't my body caressed by your fingers!" She feels hurt and angry, and her eyes are moist with tears. The man is silent, like a statue of stone.

"It's a shock, isn't it?" she asks again in a tearful voice.

"Yes!" He sighs. The woman's face grows dim before his eyes.

"You used to say once that the child growing in its mother's womb is the loveliest creation in the universe, didn't you?"

"Yes!" He keeps gazing into space with a death-like, glazed look.

"Then why does it shock you to hear of this baby? Don't you realize that the dream of this child is imbued with drops of my blood?" She covers her eyes to hide her tears.

Again a long silence – the man keeps his gaze on her.

"Just listen to me." The woman doesn't answer him (the sound of a sob). He takes hold of the hand which is covering her eyes and whispers, "Listen! In this hell, where man is devouring man, and death has spread its wings everywhere, what right have we to give birth to another human being?"

The woman's eyes are filled with bewilderment, as if she doesn't understand his words.

"I'm thinking of the child living inside your body. Will he be born just to die burning in a horrible war of this explosive age? And look at the hunger in this world! Do you wish to add one more name to the list of children dying of starvation!"

"Stop it!" She chokes on the scream of pain and rage rising within her.

"Let me speak! You don't realize how this world will turn into an inferno and how worthless and ghastly death will be! We shall live and die being slowly poisoned, and nowhere shall we find a safe haven for our running, bloodied feet – nowhere!"

"You're crazy to say that!"

"*You* are the crazy one who will not adjust to the savage dance of this fire, and you'll either go mad or kill yourself and yet you want to give birth to him! Are you listening to me?"

"I need strength just to listen to you, and I can't pretend I have it.'

He laughs for no reason in answer and, for a moment, the woman takes it for a moan. "I have no strength either and that's why you think I'm crazy. But don't push him towards death."

"Then what?" The woman's voice seems to come from the valley of doom.

A long silence.

"Get rid of it." The man sighs.

She feels as though a stone has been dropped with a splash into still waters and she is encircled by spreading waves – there is no end to this river of fire.

"No, never!" She wishes to contain all the power of the earth and the sky in her scream of negation. Desert winds blow in her eyes.

"Oh!" He sighs bitterly. "You're a woman with a heart like a pearl, yet why can't you comprehend my meaning. We have time bombs tied to us and who knows when they will explode. You, I and him as well!"

Grieved, she mumbles in a melting voice, "The trouble is that the beauty within you has died, but I feel as if with his tiny feet, he is stepping into every part of my body. His hands are touching my limbs. I can feel his lips suckling from me!"

"The real trouble is that you are still forcing him down death's throat!" His laughter has the acid taste of pain and hatred. "Starvation, unemployment, fire! Wrath of God ! Defeat upon defeat! Death and destruction! He will come into the world with a begging bowl in his hand! Kneeling before the Superpowers – begging for life – begging for food – begging for the freedom to breathe – begging for everything!"

He holds her in his arms. The pain of separation flows through their bodies. The man places his lips on her full belly, holding back his tears. Distress, hatred and protest seep like poison through the woman's blood and fill her eyes. Suddenly she breaks out of the enfolding arms and gets up. The reflection of love that had been floating earlier on the surface of her eyes is replaced by tears of hatred on the tips of her eyelashes.

"No heart beats inside you. A stone sits there instead. I hate you – hate you – hate you!" She sobs convulsively.

"Are you leaving then?" He feels himself consumed in flames.

"Yes I am." Full of tears but still a gleam of hope in the woman's eyes.

"Although you know there's no hope of a safe haven anywhere?"

"A haven is inside the heart. Whoever finds security within himself realizes that the whole world offers protection." The woman raises one foot to go and something shatters in the man's heart. He obstructs her path.

"Don't leave me, please!"

"What is there left here to stop me. All the beauty of your heart is dead . . . it lies cold and you smell of destruction. Don't . . . don't glare at me with your deathly eyes."

To prevent her from giving birth to his child, he walks fast to overtake her. They are both breathing hard. She wants to get out of sight.

"Whatever happens, I'll never have an abortion. Whatever happens – never!"

The sun is setting behind the tall, shady trees. Withered, yellow leaves are falling on the dark, desolate road. Staring far into space, she says, 'You have a stone instead of a heart, but I find everything beautiful, and when he is born, it will become even more lovely."

"And when Hell explodes, then all the beauty you talk of will be instantly destroyed!" His voice is choked with poison.

"No, the sun will still rise. Every child being born is like a new sun. Let me go. You want to kill the beauty flowering within me. You must realize that if he dies without being born, the explosion of Hell will rise even higher and nobody will be left alive to extinguish it."

"This is just your dream." He smiles sorrowfully.

"I know it to be true."

"If you are determined to bear him, if you have decided to go your own separate way, then you must tell him from me that I did not wish him to be born. It is because – because – I don't want him to gasp for each breath. You will tell him this, won't you? I know that when he is born, he will hold it against you and protest against his birth, against living and dying in the flames of this fire."

She pauses for a few moments and gazes at him with tears welling in her eyes. "Listen, at this moment when your child is being nourished within my body, I feel peace all around me . . . there is endless serenity on this earth. I am the embodiment of tranquillity and my desire to live is a harbour of safety for me and my child. I trust that even beyond annihilation lies the great range of the wonder of life."

In reply, he smiles sadly. Before them lies the turning which is her own separate path.

"Farewell. You must turn back here. Don't try to follow. I am going forth in search of perfection on this wonderful earth. And one day, when your heart too is as clear as a mirror and when you have more faith in life than in death – then we'll both meet on some bend in the road."

He stands in silence. Feeling the approach of autumn, he watches her slowly disappear round the curve of the path. She is lost to his sight and, standing beneath the tree, he covers his eyes with his hand, in despair.

He feels a bomb exploding somewhere in the background and before him a woman giving birth to a child. The sound of explosions merges with the high-pitched screams of a newborn baby.

Originally translated from the Sindhi
by Razia Tatiq and Atiya Shah

Descent
Mumtaz Shirin

He looked up.

A long flight of stairs led up – broad, white and shining. White stairs leading to the white rooms upstairs bathed in light . . . the light up there.

They stood at the foot of the stairs. Both of them. He looked up at the long flight . . . no, she couldn't manage it. She couldn't climb all these steps in her condition. He said tenderly, "Let me carry you."

She blushed and shook her head, "No . . . no. Fancy carrying me all that way up . . . and people looking."

"I don't care . . ." He stretched out his arms towards her. But she pushed them aside protesting, "I can get up these stairs myself."

"All right, then, I'll just hold you for support."

He put his arm round her shoulders, holding her tight.

Together, they climbed the stairs, step by step.

The steps, broad, white, shining, led up to the white room upstairs. There was light up there, where Life was born.

Pain shot through her, now at short intervals. A few steps up and the pain became more frequent and sharp, through her spine, her hips, her belly. Cold shivers ran down her whole body, beads of perspiration stood out on her forehead. He took out a handkerchief and mopped her face. "It will be over, soon," he murmured tenderly. He held her close. "Just lean on me, put all your weight on me. There, that's right. That should help." She closed her eyes and let her head fall on his shoulder.

Step by step, they went up.

The nurses took her in; he was asked to wait outside. He sat there on a bench . . . it all seemed so sudden. He hadn't expected it yet . . . it was rather early. She had been fine that evening. He had come home as usual, dead tired, and she had greeted him with a tender, soothing smile. She was pained to see him in low spirits and worn out. As usual she had brought the pitcher and poured him water to wash his face and hands. What a dutiful wife! Feelings of love and gratitude surged up in his heart. He wished her to sit by him and talk, talk to him of the old happy days. But she said he should have his supper first; he looked so weak and exhausted. She laid out the supper. He and the children sat down to their meagre meal. She went into the kitchen, perhaps to see what else she could give them . . . and then he saw her clutch the door and sink on to the threshold. He left his food and ran to her, picking her up and carrying her to the bed. He asked anxiously what the matter was. But she wouldn't say. She was always like this, trying to hide her pain from him. But he could sense the pain . . . and then she had to admit that "it" had started . . . he had rushed off with her.

How he hoped all would be well . . . she had so shivered in his arms as he brought her up the stairs. She must be suffering terribly. So weak, she had hardly any strength left. Would she come out alive from this struggle of life and death? . . . Pain gripped his heart as he sat there, outside, waiting.

And she lay inside, in the labour ward. The pains were now unbearable. Her eyes bulged; she bit her lips hard. But she didn't moan, she wouldn't let a single cry escape her lips. For he would know by her moaning that she was suffering terribly and he would suffer, too. She didn't utter a sound, she just suffered and suffered, until she could suffer no more. She lost consciousness.

He stood by the closed door, possessed by a kind of madness. He paced up and down; then returning to the bench he sat, fidgeting restlessly. He stared into empty space with eyes that saw nothing. But his ears strained hard to catch the faintest moan or cry from the labour ward. Not a sound could be heard. All was still. Could it mean . . . ? He felt a stab at his heart. "O, God, God! Let her live," he prayed silently from the depths of his soul. There was a saying that it almost cost the mother her own life to bring new life into the world. He strained his ears again. All was still as before.

Maybe she was bearing it with patience, just as she had always borne it with patience. Maybe she was alive, and all was well.

He sat there on the bench, waiting and waiting, endlessly it seemed. Time stood still. The suffering, the pain, the torture of a lifetime was poured into those few moments.

But, inside, she lay there still unconscious . . . It was a very tiny baby and before the cord could even be cut from its navel, it was no more. Slowly, she gained consciousness. She didn't ask about the baby. Some secret, unknown, vague feeling, a "sixth sense", had warned her it was dead. The nurses comforted her. She shouldn't worry, it was always so with babies born in the eighth month . . . they rarely lived. One of the nurses brought the baby and held it out for her to see. Slowly, she turned her head sideways. Just one look at that tiny pale face, that tiny lifeless body, and two silent tears flowed down her cheeks. And the warm flow of motherly love that began to surge in her breast anew ran cold within her.

The door opened and a nurse came out. He jumped to his feet and stared madly at the nurse. The baby had died as soon as it was born, she said . . . he shouldn't worry . . . it was always so with babies born in the eighth month. But he wasn't thinking of the baby. Only whether she was alive . . . was she? The nurse went on, "Don't you worry. These babies rarely live."

"But what about my wife?"

"Your wife? Well, why don't you get her a cup of coffee? That will perk her up a bit."

Coffee for his wife? So she was alive, then.

When he came back with the coffee, he found she had been taken to another ward where she was lying quietly on the bed. He stood next to her, watching her pale, weak body.

"How are you feeling now?" he asked her softly, taking her cold, perspiring hand in his.

She smiled faintly, "I am all right. But this time I was too weak, you know. Every joint in my body aches."

They didn't speak of the baby. He thought it was better this way. She had survived, and that was all he had wished for.

The next morning he went back to the hospital, bringing the children with him. She smiled at them. They gathered round their mother's bed while he sat next to her, holding her hand in his.

Catching the anxious look in his eyes, she pressed his hand in reassurance. Her eyes rested on his face. There was such a wealth of tenderness and affection in them . . . such love, devotion and silent worship.

Neither he nor she was the least bit attractive now: his shapeless clothes hung loosely about his dark, bony form, while hers were coarse and faded. She had lost her figure from bearing child after child, and both were worn out by hard work. Their good looks had gone: poverty had snatched what little charm youth had lent. Once wheat-brown, he had now turned quite dark-skinned. His cheeks were all sunk in. Her complexion was a very pale yellow with dark rings around her eyes that were sunk deep into their sockets. Hardly twenty-five, she looked already aged. She was just wasting away. But something apart from beauty, a force stronger than physical attraction, had drawn these two so close together. From the moment the elders had joined their hands according to religious rites they had belonged to one another. She knew she should love her husband: he was her lord and she should worship him. So she loved him, worshipped him and devoted her life to his service.

And for his part he was aware that a weak, delicate being had been given into his care, that he should protect and support her. This weak being would share her life with him, would be mistress of his house, mother of his children. And thus their hearts had come together. Long communion had helped make them what they were; it had deepened their affection and love for each other. And the children born of their love cemented the bond.

The children sensed, too, that all was not well with their mother. Anxiously they enquired, "Mother, are you ill?" and laid their foreheads on hers. "Is it fever?" And the youngest one said so touchingly, "Which place hurts you, Mum? Show me; I'll kiss it there and make the pain go away . . ." He kissed her arms, "Here?" She held her little one, clasping him to her heart. She felt so very, very happy. How they loved her . . . her little ones, her very own flesh of her flesh, blood of her blood. She had given them her life-blood to make them grow. These little beings who had taken their shape and their life within her womb . . . she sighed at the thought that she had failed to create a new life, this time.

What else, after all, was there in her dreary, miserable life of poverty, starvation, misery, grief, pain – but the children who loved her, the husband who cared for her? Yes, these were the treasures of her life.

Visitors' time was up and they had to leave.

She followed them all the way with her eyes as they went down the ward and out of the door.

The next morning he came back to find her lying quiet and calm. But she was paler then ever. Her face was as yellow as if it had been sprinkled with turmeric water. She looked as though all the blood had been drained out of her body.

A nurse came in and pricked her thumb to take a drop of blood. She soaked it on paper to gauge the haemoglobin. Just then the lady doctor entered the ward. She examined it and turned on him almost in fury. "Can't you see the danger your wife is in?"

She said in English, "Don't you realize why? You never gave her liver extract injections, you never gave her tonics while she was pregnant. And now, when she's beyond all hope of recovery, you bring her in here. And, I suppose, you're now going to blame us when she dies."

Every word uttered by the lady doctor struck him like the blow of a hammer. He did not love his wife? He did not care for her? He never gave her tonics and injections? . . . A petty clerk. How was he supposed to afford tonics and injections for his wife? And now she was reduced to this terrible condition . . . close to death . . . close to death . . . Oh, what Hell it was, this poverty.

So he stopped going to his office by bus, and walked all the way instead. He gave up smoking his cheap cigarettes. And with the few *annas* that he managed to save, he bought her fruits. He borrowed the money to pay for her injections.

But still she lay there pale and weak as ever, a most deathly pale. Her face was bleached white. Her body was cold and numb. Warm leather gloves and stockings were drawn on to her hands and legs, and hot water bottles and bags were placed under her feet. One could sense something invisible hovering over her – some foreboding of death.

Yet, she always had a faint, reassuring smile for him. As he sat nearby, looking at her, pain was reflected in his eyes. He comforted her. "You'll soon get well. I'll take good care of you. I'll get you tonics and fruit. I am managing to save some money, you know." And very sadly she smiled at him. 'Yes, I'll soon get well" – a ray of hope. Maybe this hope would keep the flame of her life alight. But the next moment he realized that her smile was forced, and her eyes had a faraway look.

And then came the critical night. Her calmness gave way to groans. All that night she moaned and groaned ceaselessly, piteously. He saw the crisis ahead. He begged of the nurses and the doctors to let him stay with her, just one night. They turned deaf ears to his entreaties. It was against the hospital rules! Anyway, this wasn't a Special Ward where people could stay with the patient! A nurse came in to give her tablets to help her sleep. She shouted brutally, "Can't you be quiet? Your groaning's horrible. Don't you realize the patients in other wards are being disturbed?"

The patients in the "other wards". Why couldn't she come out with the whole truth? . . . The patients in the "special wards" . . . "the chosen few" – and he had to put up with this treatment because he was poor, not one of "the chosen few", he thought bitterly as he plodded home. Her groans haunted him. And as he himself lay wide awake, staring at the ceiling, he could hear that piteous moaning all night long.

Next morning she was calm once again. Did it mean the crisis had passed, he thought hopefully. But the lady doctor examined her and shook her head in despair.

"There is only one hope left."

"What is it, doctor?" he asked wildly.

"Blood transfusion . . ."

"Please test my blood, doctor, see if it suits her . . ."

The doctor looked this man up and down from his head to his feet . . . He wanted to give his blood, this lean, lanky man? He seemed to have very little of it himself. But his beseeching, melting look seemed to say that he did.

"Take any amount of blood, if it will save her life." A few hundred cc's of blood were drawn from his body and transfused into her body. As her husband's blood, every drop of which contained the warmth of his love, passed through her veins, she gained a little warmth. She seemed to revive. He touched her head. It was warm . . . it was warm. He bent over her and whispered, softly, "You will recover now, surely you will." She gave him a warm smile. She had understood everything. She thanked him with her "yes". And she opened her lips to say something, but her lips trembled, she turned blue and her whole body passed through violent convulsions that shook it all over. She dug her nails into the sheets. He caught hold of her and bent over her. She wished to say something. But her lips just parted and trembled. Perhaps she was asking for her children . . . In his distress, this was the thought that flashed in his mind. He asked his next-door neighbours, who had come with him that day, to go and get the children. Their house was not far off and they were soon brought back. She looked at them one by one. She tried to stretch her arms out towards the youngest one but her arms fell, lifeless. She looked at him for the last time, as though bidding him good-bye.

And then, it was all over.

Beating his head he called out to her, called her name, over and over. But then he realized he was in the hospital. He should not behave in this way. And there were the children: he should keep calm before them. He let himself fall on to a chair. The children stood by their father's chair, staring at their mother's body. The mystery of death was beyond their understanding.

He sat staring at her too, while the nurses spread white sheets over her. White sheets, and a face as white as those sheets. White face and thick black hair falling on to her shoulders. He stared and stared.

Oblivious to his surroundings, he caught faintly, very faintly, a few words that were being spoken around him. It was the lady doctor who was saying, "It's too late tonight. You may take the body home tomorrow. Meanwhile the corpse will be kept in the mortuary. We're sorry we couldn't save her . . . you can pay the bill later . . ."

But the women from the lowest class, who bore the corpses down, started shrieking: "We won't take it down unless we're paid first."

And he heard the nurses muttering to each other:

"Well, we've all seen plenty of deaths in here. A dead body's never scared us – we're used to it. But just look at her . . . don't you feel . . . ?" They whispered something to each other.

They were insulting her even in death.

Suddenly, he rose to his feet and lifted the body up in his arms. Somebody offered him the stretcher but he pushed it aside. And passing all those people who stood staring at him in astonishment and shock, he carried her body out to the stairs which led down to the backyard.

Just a few days before – how many days was it – he had brought her up those stairs, supporting her, holding her tight, he had made her ascend those stairs, and now, bearing her lifeless body on his arms, he was going down them again.

Once there had been life in this body. Why, even a few moments ago. Now it was cold and stiff and heavy in death. He had loved this body, loved it for ten years, and now she was lost to him forever. How often had he taken this body in his arms; when it was light and soft and warm? She was hardly fourteen years old when she had come to him as a bride. His mother was still alive then. She had made her work all day long. But when his mother went out visiting relatives they would have a wonderful time. He would lift her in his arms and whirl her round. Those happy days had come to an end all too soon. Hard work and childbearing had weakened her; she was constantly ill. He implored her not to work so hard, but she wouldn't listen. Sometimes when she was hard at work, he would creep up behind her stealthily, lift her gently up and lay her on her bed so she might rest. Yes, so often. And now he was bearing this body in his arms for the last time.

Down, down the stairs he carried her.

The stairs were narrow and dark. There was darkness all about him. The darkness of night, the darkness of Death. The steps seemed never-ending. A long way down . . . down, down. A long descent. The last descent.

Originally translated from the Urdu
by the author

Banishment
Jamila Hashmi

Bhai used to say, "*Bibi*, why do you dream all the time? This affection which you now enjoy, this light which surrounds you, will slowly fade away. Time is all-consuming. It devours everything. But the process is so gentle, so steady, we get used to it unconsciously."

Where is *Bhai* today? Where is my dear brother? If the wind and the air, my constant companions who travel everywhere with me, heavy with the fragrance of homeland, could transcend space and seek him out, I would ask, "Go and find out. Why does this anguish never diminish? Even after carrying this burden for so many years, traversing difficult paths, why do we dream? Why do we entertain hope, and long for happiness? Why do we love light so much?"

The *Seetaji* of Hindu mythology had done this too. After enduring the pain of exile, she had prayed for a reunion with her beloved husband, *Ramchandra*, so there could be light in her life. Does misfortune make us so tough and disillusioned that we forsake all hope of better days? Why can darkness not be loved? Why not?

The *naakh* tree has come into blossom every spring since the year Munni, my daughter, was born. When the seasons change, the branches are first laden with flowers; later, with the weight of its fruit, the tree droops low. This link between the tree and the soil which sustains it runs deep. Its roots go deeper and deeper into the earth. No one can break this bond. Munni has grown up now. Treading softly, time has passed me by; I often wonder at its heartlessness.

Only this morning *Badi Ma,* the grandmother, had said to Gurpal, "Son, take *Bahu* and the children to *Dasehra.* Let them enjoy the festivities. For so many years she has not left the village."

Gurpal had snapped back quickly, "When did you ever ask me before, *Ma?* If she hasn't gone out for so many years, it's not my fault."

I listen to their conversation in silence. It cannot be anyone's fault. But it's strange that whenever someone calls me *Bahu,* as if I really am a daughter-in-law, I feel as though I am being abused. I have been used to abuse for many years now, ever since that dreadful night when Gurpal had shoved me in through the courtyard and announced proudly, "Look here, *Ma,* I have brought a daughter-in-law for you. Young, charming and healthy. She is the best of the bunch of girls we got our hands on tonight."

Badi Ma, his grandmother, was sitting on the wooden couch. She had listened to him silently, without even a flicker of surprise. Then she had got and picked up the earthen lamp. With slow steps she had come over to me, raised high the flame of the lamp and stood scrutinizing me. Her eyes roved insolently over my face as if I were not a human being but a new animal which her grandson had acquired for her.

I could hardly keep my eyes open from hunger, fright and fatigue. But the knowledge of my impending doom forced me to gaze at her, wide-eyed. After walking barefoot, miles and miles through the wilderness, I had no strength left even to lift a finger. When she tried to touch me, I collapsed at her feet. As I fell I had the eerie feeling that the cow and the buffalo tied to wooden pegs in the courtyard were gazing at me despondently. Earlier, seeing me in that dreadful plight, they had stopped eating and stood up in order to look at me.

Oblivious to my plight, *Badi Ma* had picked me up roughly, examined me carefully several times from head to toe and said, "Son, if you had behaved well and done what you should, I wouldn't be in the state I'm in now. I have almost gone blind trying to feed you and fill your belly. It hasn't been easy for me to keep the hearth burning. Even the *kaharis* have stopped coming here because we don't offer them grain at harvest time. Tell me, son, how can I bear the burden of running this house? Instead of indulging in all sorts of adventures, why don't you till our small piece of land? That would give me some sort of relief."

Gurpal had listened to her and then replied gently, "Now stop it. Look, now there'll be no need to put up with the piggishness of *kaharis* and *mehris,* those menial women. You'll have a maid-servant of your own from now on. Make her grind the millstone and fetch water from the well. You can order her to do anything you want. That's not my domain. I have brought a real *Bahu* for you, *Ma!*"

Since that fateful night, many daughters-in-law had been brought to this village. But there were no festivities. No music was played nor did village belles sing joyous marriage songs to the accompaniment of the *dholak.* And the dancers did not perform.

That night no one applied oil to my dust-covered hair. No one dressed me up for my wedding night. With bare, unadorned hands I became a bride and without any ceremony my marriage was consummated. Overnight I became Maaji's *Bahu.* No one blessed me! No ritual offerings were made to the poor!

On the contrary, after listening to Gurpal, *Badi Ma* had looked at me with disgust as if I were an affliction, as if her grandson had kidnapped and dragged home something repulsive. Holding the flickering lamp in one hand, she had quietly gone back to the kitchen with a frown on her wrinkled forehead. In that telling moment no one had commented: how shameful it was to welcome the *Bahu* in this manner!

Since then I too have become a *Seeta*. I too have suffered the pangs of banishment and been imprisoned in Sangraon.

Dismantling the swings which had been set up for the fair, the *beedi*-smoking owners are swearing at each other in their usual way. In their attempt to leave the place as fast as possible, they are loading their paraphernalia roughly on to their donkeys as if these beasts of burden were made of wood. The chariots which were used for the festival of *Ramlila* are now parked on one side and the youngsters who had participated in this folk drama are gobbling up ice-cream and savoury foods, ignoring the bustle around them. The ugly stains of the candy and the sauce on their colourful costumes look like the sores of leprosy.

Munni is standing gazing at them with interest. My innocent Munni. The danger of getting lost in the mad rush of that jostling crowd doesn't worry her. Is it any use being aware of danger, I wonder. If someone is destined to get lost, he or she will, inevitably. Even from the safety of a house bursting with people.

Gurpal spots her and drags her away from the vendors. But the two tired boys are insisting on buying something from every vendor they come across. After all, it is festival time and this is a gay, noisy fair. Here, unbothered by the safety of their children, mothers are being hustled and bumped from side to side, and their wailing brats are continuously being pushed forward, in an effort to keep an eye on them. Those who get lost during such fairs, what happens to them? Are they ever found? They are never seen again. This abstract contemplation, this strange feeling of alienation which develops in those who have never gone through this hell, becomes a barrier even between sworn lovers. The faces of those near and dear ones, for even one glimpse of whom we would gladly sacrifice all our wordly goods, are never seen again.

Suddenly the tracks behind us are obliterated like the marks of insects on restless waves of shifting sand; like languid streams of reminiscences that cross and cross again and get mixed up slowly with a faint sound like suppressed weeping. The roads we have trodden disappear and we find it impossible to go back the way we came. Nothing ever comes back and the seething crowd which had gathered to enjoy the festivities of the fair moves forward, on and on. Time never returns, never retraces its steps. *Bhayya* used to say, "*Bibi,* that moment of time which has gone by is effaced. It becomes dust." He used to tell me that, whenever I failed to attend to my studies and played with my doll's house instead.

That doll's house was a gift from father. He had bought it for me at some exhibition.

Now Munni is holding her large rag doll in her two little hands. While Gurpal is still watching the movements of the happy crowd, Munni is caressing her doll and looking anxiously at it as if she were worried about its safety. Both the boys have managed to get statues of *Rawan,* the incarnation of evil. Fascinated by the pageantry around them, they gaze in amazement at every face that comes near. Munni's bright eyes are full of love for her ugly doll. On its broad face, a grotesque nose and eyes have been embroidered with big, clumsy stitches. There is a nose ring in one of her nostrils. This metal ring has given her the status of a virgin. With a golden-laced headcloth covering its head, the doll is carefully holding the lower garment wound around her waist. In this posture, the doll looks like a dancer about to begin a dance.

We have a long way to go yet. We have to tread the track which passes by the banks of Uchchal's pond. Then it crosses some fields and takes us to Sangraon, our village. Thus the caravan of life goes on. Even if there is no will, no longing to reach a destination, it goes on along straight and winding roads, semi-dark, criss-crossing footpaths through strange lanes and side lanes and you have to drag your tired feet on continually. Even if your feet are bruised and you have nothing, no desire in your heart, you have to keep walking, walking, endlessly.

The bluish mist of twilight has now descended over us from the canopy of the heavens. God knows why the evenings always sadden me. Far up in the sky, the lonely star is twinkling like the filament of an earthen lamp, and in the misty tinge of the empty sea around me, its loneliness reminds me of my penal banishment. In this human wilderness, I suddenly feel as though I am a lonely tree which neither blossoms nor bears fruit.

The lonesome star reminds me of the ship in which my brother went to sea. When he was getting ready to go to some far-off land, mother's voice had become choked with grief. But with great strength and steadiness, she had arranged everything for him and packed his belongings. And all the while, she had silently prayed. Outside, father was busy looking after the other arrangements. *Bhai,* despite the excitement of travelling to foreign lands, looked sad and depressed. *Apa* too was busy. Saying nothing she padded silently from one part of the house to the other. It was only I who warbled excitedly all over the house. It was natural. Unless you are wounded yourself, how can you feel the pain of injury?

We had gone to the port to see him off. *Bhayya* was going up and down the gangway supervising the carting of his younger brother's luggage. Since I had nothing much to do, I had gone to the guard-rail. Resting my hands on it, I stooped to gaze into the greenish, muddy water below. Then suddenly I had asked my brother, "Why is the water so peculiar? How is it that there are large oil stains on it? What is the secret of those mysterious boats and why those paddles? And why these anchors? When these boats swing and tremble, tossing on the wavering waves, don't you feel frightened?"

Questions, innumerable questions. They often bothered me. That day, distressed by the barrage of my questions, my brother had replied, "Don't be impatient, *Bibi.* When you grow up, you'll know the answers. Then you'll understand everything."

And now I have learnt many things. I have the answers to all my questions. I know what happens to boats. That a boat which doesn't have oars sinks. Boats can sink even on the shores of rivers and seas and oceans. Just one wave is sufficient to drown it, you don't need a whole ocean. Having grown up, I know these secrets. Alas, *Bhai* is not with me now.

That day each one of us was lost in thought. Suddenly, when we heard the wailing whistle of the ship, we realized that *Bhai* was about to leave. *Baba* embraced him warmly. Placing his hand on *Bhai*'s head, he blessed him, "Well, I entrust you to Allah." *Bhayya* also embraced him lovingly. *Apa* had always been soft-hearted; she cried on almost every occasion. That day too she began to cry. *Bhai* consoled her, saying, "Look at *Bibi*, how happy she is. Why these tears? I'll be back in two years. I'm not leaving you for good. Come on, dry your tears and wish me goodbye with smiles." Then reaching out to me, took me tenderly in his arms and said, "You're a brave girl, *Bibi*. I'll bring you beautiful gifts from Paris. Keep in touch and write to me regularly." And I nodded obediently.

When we heard the last whistle of the ship, he left us, walking casually as if he were on his way to some nearby city. After he went we stayed there waving our handkerchiefs till the ship was out of sight. Then in the twilight, when the bright lights of the port began to shimmer in the restless waves of the sea and the beacon lights of the ship twinkled like the lonely star in the heavens above and then disappeared into the far-off mists, suddenly all the lights around me were drowned forever. That was the beginning of the end. After that night, not one ray of light has ever come out of the waves for me.

The memory of that day is still fresh in my mind. Watching the ship disappear over the horizon, I felt something strange inside me. Embracing my mother suddenly, I screamed out loud. I felt as though my heart was telling me that I would never see my dear brother again. You will never see him again, *Bibi*. With the ominous message, my heart had begun to pound wildly. Just like the frightened, lonesome star in the empty sky, trembling in the bluish twilight.

In the distant gardens, the darkness of the night is spreading its wings slowly. Gurpal has picked up both his sons and is now carrying them on his shoulders. He is walking ahead of us on the narrow track winding like a white line, a sort of giant ribbon, through the fields. Munni and I are walking wearily. After jumping over several canals, he will cross the fields and then wait for us. And to while away the time, he will narrate the story of *Rawan,* who kidnapped *Seeta.* He is not aware that *Seeta* is walking right behind him and that he himself is *Rawan*!

While I am lost in the swelling tide of memories, Munni suddenly says, "Ma, Saroop's uncle has sent beautiful clothes for *Dasehra.* They are all made of silk. It feels so good to touch them. Ma, don't I have an uncle to send me nice gifts? Where is my uncle, Ma? Why don't you reply, Ma? Why are you so silent? Didn't you like the fair? I think you are very tired, aren't you, Ma?"

"Yes, Munni, I am exhausted," I reply softly. And then I add, "I have also grown old."

Munni looks at me surprised, and then smiles and says with great confidence, "Old? No, no, Ma. You look just like the image of the goddess which I have seen in the village. *Badi Ma* also says you are a *devi.*"

Munni is so young. She doesn't know the distance I have had to walk to get this far. She is also not aware that the distance between one life and another is so vast, so immeasurable. And when someone writhes and loses hope and has no longing in his heart, that is when he becomes fit to be worshipped. On the pathways of Sangraon, while waiting ardently for my lost ones, my eyes have lost their light and become dim with expectation. My heart is void of all feeling – it is empty.

Munni is once again asking me, "Ma, don't we really have an uncle?"

I look at her vaguely. What should I say? What should I tell her? Standing at crossroads, I begin to think.

Bhayya was so dear to me. But I was afraid of him. Whenever he came into the house, my headcloth used to go over my head as if by itself. In front of him I used to walk gently and speak softly. Whenever I stood by him, I used to think: no one can be taller than him. My Bhayya, who walked carefully and talked gracefully and wrote with such a beautiful hand, neat and straight. He neither spoiled the pages of his notebooks nor stained his hands with ink. I could never be as neat as him. Whenever I felt depressed, he used to encourage me, "Don't worry, Bibi. When you grow up, you too will write neatly like me."

God knows what Bhayya, who loved to write neatly without blots, would say if he could see me now. My Book of Destiny is soiled and there is black ink all over its pages. There is not one straight line on any page. I could never learn to write neatly. In those days, after arranging the furniture in my doll's house, I used to think: it's so spacious. Surely we can all live in it. Ammah and Baba and I and Bhayya and Bhai and Apa, everyone. We will all live here peacefully. Life is a sonorous, happy song. We shall need and want for nothing.

When Bhayya got married, I had said: our house is a heaven. A complete divine house of bliss. In those days, had I raised my hands to pray, I wouldn't have known what to pray for. There was nothing that I needed. There was nothing to pray for, to invoke the blessings of Allah. Just as now, even in those days I never asked anything of Allah. How strange that in the whirlpool of life, the pinnacle of both happiness and suffering occurs at the same point.

Bhai went overseas and the dream of my heaven was shattered. The splinters of life, like sharp slivers of glass, get scattered everywhere. They injure passers-by, crippling their feet. No one may cross the road, escape to the other side. The road itself is so desolate. It looks as though it winds across a cremation ghat. It is so quiet and eerie, I cannot see anyone, anywhere, not even on

the far horizon. In such morbid surroundings, in such a bleak
land, who listens to the wails of *Seetaji?* The pain of solitude and
loneliness is cruel. How hard life is.

Standing far away, Gurpal is now calling me loudly. He
is also calling Munni. But we continue to walk slowly. In the
cotton fields, only the stubble remains. People have picked all the
flowers. In the wheat fields, the ears have not yet appeared and
there is no grain. The breeze is strong and gusts of wind bend the
pliant plants. When it is blows hard you have to stoop. Everyone
stoops low when facing the wind.

By now *Badi Ma* must be restless. Even worried. God knows
why she is always anxious about me, as though she were smitten
by some unknown fear. The road which goes from here to that
country which so scares her is full of hazards. And the road on
which I have travelled with Gurpal, I do not have the strength
to venture beyond it. How far can you walk, particularly when
you have no place to go? With blistered feet and a wounded
heart, a despoiled womanhood, where can I go? How could
I go anywhere? Munni stands in my way. Between them and
me, Munni is the thick veil. The distance between them and
me is so great, the gap between us so wide. How can I peep
beyond it?

Several groups of wandering minstrels are coming up behind
us, singing devotional songs. The fair had almost got stuck for
several hours near the Uchchal pond. Now it has thinned out
and the crowd has dispersed and spread along the roads and
crossroads. Tired children are wailing, and noisy men, talking
loudly and laughing, have just passed by Munni and me. They are
being followed by barefoot, colourfully dressed village women
whose heads are partially covered with veils. Holding bundles of
sweets bought at the fair, with their little children clinging on to
them, they are walking briskly. To keep up their pace they have
removed their shoes and tied them to their head-dresses. Each one
of them has this bundle dangling behind.

The men who passed us are now far away, they look like white spots. I can hear a holy man playing his single stringed instrument. He too is walking on the track which goes to Sangraon. There is pathos in the music of this instrument and in the droning of the accompanying song. These folk songs deal with life. The singer is right. When there is no sign of fight, when it doesn't exist, even then one longs for it. Is it because one is frightened of darkness?

Now I can no longer hear the vibrations of his string clearly. But occasionally, on a gust of wind, the words of his song reach my ears. Suddenly Munni asks, "Ma, why are you so quiet? Please keep on talking, Ma. I am scared." In the deepening darkness, she tries to hold my hand hard. But in doing so, she loses her grip on the doll and drops it. She picks it up quickly and looks distressed. I can feel her voice is steeped in tears and she is in no state to ask more questions.

When she grows up Munni will also learn that it is futile to be frightened of darkness. It overpowers you. You can do nothing. *Bhai* used to say, "*Bibi*, running water has great force. It carves out its own passage." What did he mean by that? Is running water as devastating as darkness?

Whenever *Badi Ma* calls me, I cover my forehead with my headcloth. "Yes," I reply softly. "Yes, *Badi Ma*." Then I try to remain so busy with my daily chores throughout the day that I have no time to remember my loneliness, and learn to live with the darkness around me.

When there was time to contemplate, there was nothing to think about. Now I have lots to muse on, but there isn't any time. Everywhere, something is always lacking, something missing. The feeling of paucity is always there. Nothing ever happens to bring me peace. Today, as I close my eyes, my heart whispers: they will all come back. As soon as *Bhayya* sees me he will say, "*Bibi*, what is this charade? What is this disguise? This veil on your face and this covering on your head. It doesn't look nice. Throw it away,

Bibi, and see what I have brought for you. Stop all your work.
No more chores for you. Come and sit near me. Holidays are rare
and they end quickly. When I am home, don't go out anywhere."

Sitting comfortably on the sofa in our drawing room, with
large photographs around us, or down near the fireplace where
we usually sat in winter, talking about everything on earth, we
often laughed noisily, as if life was continuous laughter. We
talked till late into the night. Disturbed in her sleep, mother used
to chide drowsily, "For God's sake, go to bed, children. You
have to get up early." On such occasions, it was *Bhayya* who
used to reply loudly, "I spend so much time away from home,
Ammah. All through the year I fall asleep sad and lonely. Let
us enjoy ourselves now. What's the rush? We will sleep when
we are sleepy."

At such times I used to think (though God knows why):
all these happy moments will vanish. They will disappear as
everything does, into the dust. The haven we have lovingly built
will also be covered by dust storms and there will be no freshness
or greenery anywhere. We are but shadows, like photographs
on our walls. I was always crazy. Also foolish. Always lost in
enigmatic, morbid thoughts.

Perhaps I have not changed even now. The heart forever
dreams of impossible things. Whenever I try to confide my
dreams, it says: what does it matter, *Bibi?* There is no controlling
dreams. And what's wrong with your dream of seeing them all
some day walking in through the open door? Aren't they your
loved ones, for whose coming you have waited so ardently?

Confused and uncertain, I reply: for me nothing remains
except gloom and the murk of darkness.

This doesn't convince my heart; it once had smelt the familiar
fragrance in the gusts of hope.

What should I hope for? Munni has caught hold of my
dress. She is asking me, "Ma, what has happened to our uncle?
Why doesn't he ever come to see us? Shall we not visit him on this

Divali either? All the girls visit an uncle's house at Divali time. That's why I am so sad, Ma. Take me to uncle's house at least once."

I listen to her silently. Where is her uncle's house? Whom should I ask? In which town? All the villages outside Sangraon look like doll's houses to me. They are not real. Sangriton is also a shadow. Everything around me is a large shadow. Dark, silent, and mysterious. Even then I do not know why this restless soul of mine continues to wander. It probes into events, tries to search for objects which never existed. Longs to listen to voices which will never be heard again.

Carrying baskets of cow-dung on my head, milking cows and buffaloes, making cow-dung cakes, for fuel. I feel my heart pound so sickeningly, God knows why. Suddenly I can smell the familiar fragrance in the gusts of breeze. Suddenly I can hear the musical notes I remember so well. Now I know the secret of these strange feelings. These cruel sensations which took me away from my own self. But it is different now that I know the truth. The bitter truth. I know where my loved ones are. That land is beyond my reach. Like the roads to Sangraon, these winding, twisting tracks crossing each other move on and on and vanish into oblivion. What could I do to locate this focus of my dreams, this city of my fables?

Through the open doors of homes, lights from the flickering flames of lamps look like pictures from a mysterious fairyland. Gurpal and the boys, Munni and I, we are all walking side by side. A breeze full of silken husks from the reeds of the adjoining fields is playing with my dusty hair. The evening looks sleepy and dull. If you have company the journey becomes light.

Munni is complaining, "Ma, I am exhausted. I can't walk any more." The boys are crying. Their eyes too are heavy with sleep. We leave the track and rest for a while on the ridge of a field. Gurpal says, "Look how foolish those women were. So many children got lost today. They foolishly lose themselves at the fair. In the frenzy of enjoyment, mothers get separated from their children. Aren't they crazy?"

"Children get lost even apart from fairs, don't they?" I said without looking at him, and caressing Munni.

"Won't you ever forget all that? Those were different days. It's different now," Gurpal replies softly.

How could I forget? How could I explain to Gurpal that time never changes. It's always the same. There is pain and anguish in one's destiny because one cannot forget. Those wretched days are still alive in my memory with all their vividness. A fire was raging everywhere. The country was partitioned. *Ammah* and *Baba* said, "All these people have lost their heads. They are frightened for nothing. That's why they are running away to another country. In the midst of so many dear ones, how can anyone inflict pain on us?"

How simple and innocent they were. Pain is always inflicted by the near and dear ones. That distress which strangers impose has no reality. On the eve of independence, life lost its beauty and human blood began to flow on the roads. In the name of *Bhagwan, Guru* and *Allah,* people cut each other's throats. Those who were ready to die to save the honour of their mothers and sisters and daughters started regarding woman's chastity and honour as a myth. *Ammah* had told *Baba,* "Let us take our girls and migrate, I am terrified." But father had calmly replied, "You are needlessly losing your nerve. How can anyone hurt us? Partition was inevitable. Within a few days this unrest will subside. Don't worry, everything will be all right soon."

Usually such reassurances used to placate mother. But that day, she looked worried. She said, as if unconvinced, "Not only life but honour too is at stake. We have two grown daughters. Listen to me, and send them to my brother across the border."

"The journey is not safe these days. Vagabonds have taken over all the routes to Pakistan. Even the trains are not safe. Have courage and stay at home. Allah will protect us."

I am certain he too was worried, though he tried to keep up an appearance of calm. But he did not realize that time was merciless; it marched on stealthily. *Baba*'s fault was that he failed to grasp the true significance of those bloody events around him. He paid the penalty. When Gurpal was dragging me out of the house, I saw his grey head lying near the gutter. His body had been thrown in the drain. Oblivious to his closed eyes and bloodstained head, the others kept on praying fervently to God. That was not the time to invoke Allah's blessings. Just then a gleaming spear went through *Ammah*'s heart and she dropped dead instantly on the very spot where minutes earlier she had been praying ardently for the safety of her daughters and her own honour, and protection from marauders.

Even now, in the noise of stormy nights, I can hear *Apa*'s shrieks. I was as helpless then as I am now. Gurpal was dragging me brutally with him. I had no cover on my head. There was no chance of coming across *Bhayya* on the way. Had he been with me, who would have dared to touch me? No one could ever dream of kidnapping me on the streets of my motherland, every particle of which was dear to me. Those streets which had been soaked in my father's blood. That dust in which his grey head had fallen. Where is that land, my motherland? If I can only glimpse its soil I will pick it up with veneration and kiss it reverently and hold it to my forehead. O soil, O dust of that land, you are more fortunate than I!

I had a million things to say to *Baba*. All my life I had teased *Ammah* so much. Had not spared even *Bhayya* and *Bhai*. And that dreadful night when I was dragged to Sangraon without the traditional carriage, not one of my brothers was there to bid me goodbye. How could I complain? To whom could I cry that I was leaving the land of my parents, the house where I had grown up, when there was no one to send me off.

In my new home, I had endured pain and hunger and *Badi Ma*'s beatings and Gurpal's abuses in the hope that some day

Bhayya or *Bhai* might come to Sangraon looking for me. Then I would look benevolently at *Badi Ma* and, without a glance at Gurpal, go back with my brother. That day, a joyous breeze flirting exuberantly with the *peepal* leaves would sing bright songs of reunion and the whole village would rejoice. I do not know why man considers himself the centre of this universe!

In the midst of hope and despair, suddenly there had been peace between the two countries. It made Gurpal very sad. He always looked alarmed. Often he sat in the kitchen and talked in a low voice to *Badi Ma*. They kept their conversation secret. I never knew what they talked about. In those days Munni had just started walking. For a while the news of peace circulated with excitement but then it collapsed like a whirlwind. No one came to take me back. Not even the army came to repatriate me.

Then I heard that in the nearby villages, soldiers of the other country had traced many girls and come to take them away. To which country and to which people? I did not get an answer.

In those days I too hoped: maybe soon my brothers will come looking for me. They have been waiting for me beyond the gates of the magic city for a long time. I should go. Daily I waited for them, leaning heavily on hopes and longings and gazing intently at the turning of my lane.

During the winter of that year, soldiers eventually came to Sangraon, to take me back. But as well as the beloved sister of *Bhayya* and *Bhai*, I am also Munni's mother. And then I thought: God knows who these people are who have come for me. Which country am I supposed to be being repatriated to?

For the first time in my life my faith began to dwindle. My dream city disappeared in a haze and all of a sudden I felt that my roots in the soil of Sangraon had become deeper and stronger. Who likes to wither and be destroyed? Every girl has to bid goodbye to her maternal home and move to her husband's. After marriage every bride goes somewhere. At my marriage, if I did not meet any of my brothers, so what? Gurpal had spread a red carpet of corpses for my welcome. He had set fire to our village to provide illumination for me. Running madly and shrieking, wailing people had celebrated the festivities of my marriage.

God knows how long I had gazed at the alphabets in the book Gurpal had bought for Munni. Like a flash I remembered all those stories my brother used to narrate. Once *Bhayya* had said, "*Bibi,* there are other books which contain better stories, more interesting ones. Just grow up a bit and you'll be able to read them."

Just as it happens in stories, when the army came to repatriate me, I hid myself, as the princess had done. How could I go with strangers? Why didn't my brothers themselves come? Deep down in my heart, I was deeply hurt. I feel the hurt even now.

Whenever Munni lies down beside me in the solitude of the night, she harps on the same tune, "Ma, why didn't we go to uncle's house for *Divali?* Why doesn't anyone send us sweets?"

I feel like telling her: Munni, your uncle never came searching for me. He never came to take me away. Who has so much time that he can waste it searching for someone else?

Bhayya's children must be Munni's age now. Whenever the daughters-in-law of our lane sing and dance under the shade of the *neem* tree, I remain silent. On such occasions, there is so much splendour in our courtyard. The songs of the motherland are so lilting. Seasons change. Every year, some father or some brother comes here to take some fortunate girl home. Then in excitement, bursting with happiness, Aasha, Rekha and Chandar run hither and thither. They embrace everyone before going to their mother's house. But nothing ever happens for me.

As time dragged on, *Badi Ma* began trusting me. When I broke all the links with my past, my bonds with *Badi Ma* became deeper and stronger. Now I have become her dear daughter-in-law, as auspicious as *Lakshmi,* the goddess of wealth. And when other women complain about their daughters-in-law, she talks proudly of me to make them envious.

Despite this change of attitude, I keep on dreaming. Some day, behind the wearily walking farmers who carry heavy bundles of fodder on their backs, suddenly some valiant young man will appear riding a spirited stallion and I will dash out shouting *"Bhayya, Bhayya"* and embrace him. How foolish I am. I stand at the door; for whom am I waiting? My hopes and longings have died; how long shall I have to roam about carrying their corpses? As I watch the empty and desolate cross-roads, why do my eyes fill with tears, burning and disillusioned? If these salt droplets of water fall on to Munni, she will be upset and ask at once, "Why are you weeping, Ma?"

How can I tell her why? How can I tell her of the pangs I have suffered all these long years, the reasons for my tormented pain?

Gurpal has picked up both boys on his shoulders. Munni and I are following behind. We too are going to Sangraon. Instead of being exiled for the second time, *Seeta* has bowed down before fate and accepted life with *Rawan*. From where can I muster the strength to face the risk of uncertainty for the second time, to step out of this gloom?

All the lights and lustre of life have receded far from me, as my town once had done. Even then I cannot fall in love with this darkness. God only knows why. I know I have to continue walking. Fatigue has spread like a terrible pain all over my body, every limb. Even then I have to keep on walking. In the whirligig of life, everyone is compelled to keep walking; those who live in homes and those who wander in exile. I move forward wearily, dragging my bruised feet, and I sometimes ponder. My brothers too must often be missing me, must be feeling sad and heavy-hearted for me.

My worst fears come from Munni. Tomorrow she will again ask me awkward, painful questions. And no one will be able to satisfy her. I cannot. Neither can Gurpal, nor *Badi Ma*. Why are some queries so difficult to answer?

In the long, cold, wintry nights, pain lights up bonfires, invokes bygone dreams and listens to their tales. Maybe they are true. But how can stories be true? The human heart is very stubborn. I do not know why it always recalls days which have vanished in the dark mist of the past. Is there any notion or thought beyond Sangraon? Is there any other town beyond it? In this unevenness and the ups and downs of village lanes and alleys, the smell of death mixed with the odour of grain is flowing like life's own stream. Yet another day has ended. Like gusts of wind, days and nights slowly and steadily pass by. God knows how far I have yet to go. How much more on this track.

Originally translated from the Urdu
by Anwar Enayetullah

Dilshad

Zaitoon Bano

She did not look insane, but whenever she was asked, "Dilshad! What did you do with your son?", she would answer, "Madam! I sold him."

"For how much?"

"For one *anna*, Madam!"

The questioner would think that either she was mad or the value of just one *anna* was much higher to her. How much value can just one *anna* have in our lives?

Dilshad would turn up in our street too, but not on her own. A host of children would follow her about. Some would clap, some would throw stones at her, some would pull at her clothes, and the rest would shout and hoot.

"Dilshad, where is your son?"

"*Khan*! I sold him."

"For how much?"

"*Khan*! For one *anna*."

And the children would burst into laughter. They already knew quite well that Dilshad had sold her son for one *anna*, but they would ask her the same thing over and over again.

Another proof of her madness was that she only wore a shirt. She wore just one long shirt that dropped to her ankles. She spent the nights on the wooden planks in front of the shops, and during the day wandered about from house to house. Someone would give her a loaf of bread which she would chew to pass the day and then she would go back to her makeshift bed for the night once more.

Casually, she complained, "Madam! People don't let me into their houses. They say mad ones shouldn't be allowed inside homes. And when I sleep outside on the wooden planks, those bastards tease me the whole night. To protect my honour, I have to be on the lookout the whole time."

Such pathetic complaints brought tears to people's eyes. But she would smile. She would go round repeating her complaints to everyone. Some people would feel sorry for her, but others, glancing cynically at her smile, would give their own verdict, "She's a bad woman. See how she laughs!"

But who could possibly know the sorrow and pain behind her smile? They had no idea why she laughed in this way – or how strongly unfulfilled desires and despair had gripped her heart or what those wishes were which could not be fulfilled – all were concealed by shallow laughter.

Twice I had firm proof of Dilshad's madness, yet I remained unconvinced. If she was really mad, she had not been born that way, that much I was sure of.

I had tried on several occasions to let her spend the night in our home so she could be safe from those "bastards", but my mother disagreed. "You are crazy to make friends with mad people! God forbid, you might catch it yourself."

I tried to convince my mother by insisting, "Mama! She's not mad. What makes you think so?"

Mother would retort, "Do mad people have to have horns or tails to be obvious? Isn't it a sign of insanity that she sold her son for one *anna*! She doesn't even bother to wear trousers! Don't listen to mad people. They may sometimes sound sane, but the next moment they are demented again." I had no answer.

It can pay to be curious. I wanted to know why exactly Dilshad was considered insane. What had caused it? At last I found the answer.

One day I brought her home and, at my insistence, she agreed to tell her story. She cast a puzzled look at me and started her story in a style which was anything but lunatic:

"A son is as dear to a Pukhtun woman as faith. Why would I sell my son for an *anna*? But . . . I did indeed sell my son, my Qamar Gul, for one *anna*. It's true."

A foolish smile spread across her face, and then she went on, "I belonged to Tirah. My father had sold me for fifteen hundred rupees. I lived in peace with my husband. I had three brothers-in-law but they were my husband's stepbrothers. On the death of my father-in-law, my husband became head of the house. His stepbrothers could not bear it. There were three of them and he was all alone. And . . . one day came news of his murder. He had been shot dead. By whom? It was never found out. His brothers threw all that Pukhto stood for to the wind and did not even bother to follow up the murder.

"Then I gave birth to a son, which only added to my worries and misery. The eldest brother took me in marriage by force. I was beaten mercilessly for nothing. All the chores of the household were left to me. My sisters-in-law sat around in sheer idleness, while I . . ."

She gasped in confusion, and then resumed the story.

"I was living like a slave. But I had to put up with it all purely for the sake of Qamar Gul . . . for Qamar Gul alone, Madam! He was my only remembrance of my husband. When Qamar Gul was a year and a half, the brothers fell out among themselves over the division of assets. A *jarga* proposed equal shares among the three brothers, but the eldest claimed Qamar Gul in his share as well. It was no secret the way that Qamar Gul's mother was forced to live in that house."

Dilshad related all this as if talking about someone else. She looked at me and continued, "The brothers did not say a word before the elders, but clearly considered Qamar Gul a thorn in their flesh. One day, my youngest brother-in-law attempted to pull that thorn out. He tried to choke him to death. But Qamar

Gul screamed and I reached him in time to rescue him from the clutches of death. I then realized that staying there would be very difficult, because the very life of my beloved son, and mine too, was in danger . . ."

She paused a while, as if thinking back to that horrible night.

"I slipped out of the house in the darkness of the night and made for Peshawar. In Peshawar, I had to seek charity to survive. I tried to find a job in a house but in vain. One day, I caught sight of Qamar Gul's stepfather. He was looking around impatiently, but God helped me. I turned abruptly into a street to avoid being seen. I realized they were looking for me. Neither I nor Qamar Gul was safe.

"One day, when I was on the point of collapsing with hunger, I went into a house to ask for bread. It was a rich house but there were no children. It was morning, and no food had yet been prepared. I asked for an *anna* so as to buy something in the bazaar. The mistress of the house said jokingly that if I would give her my son, she would give me one *anna*. I did not hesitate – I left her my son. I thought he would be well fed and safe. And I thought I would go there from time to time to see him alive and well. On the third day, my feelings drove me there – I had to have a look at my son. But when I got there I was informed that those people had moved to Karachi. They had taken Qamar Gul with them."

Dilshad sobbed. Her eyes were brimming and she began to stammer. I realized it was not that her face had been distorted by grief but the whole universe of a mother that had turned upside down. With great effort, she composed herself and handed me an amulet that she was wearing around her neck. "What's this?" I asked.

"Look what's in it," she said.

I opened the amulet: it was not a charm but a one-*anna* coin, and a fake one at that. I looked at the fake coin, and then at the unfortunate Dilshad, but said nothing. Perhaps Dilshad did not know the coin was not genuine, that she had sold her son for fake money. She stared about in confusion, looking as though her heart would burst or blood gush from her eyes. I had never seen her in such a state though she was trying her utmost to contain it. Finally she pulled herself together and said, "Madam! I so bitterly regret that I did not even tell that lady Qamar Gul's name, for even if they asked him, he could never tell them it himself. He was only an infant when I left him."

With these words fountains of tears flowed from her eyes. She rose and left the house.

Since then, Dilshad has never been seen around here again. God only knows whether she took herself to Karachi or wandered off somewhere else. But whenever I think of her tears, I think of the countless mad women like Dilshad roaming about in Karachi, hungry and half-naked, with "bastards" making fun of them.

Originally translated from the Pushto
by Dr Sher Zaman Taizi

A Manly Act

Neelam Ahmed Bashir

Something had to be done about Hameedan!

If the problem of Hameedan were solved, Shera and his *Ammah* would get all that their hearts desired. But to suddenly pull up a plant that had been there for years was no easy task. *Ammah* wanted him to pluck the plant out by its roots but he still had some fear of God in him. After all, he had spent so many years with Hameedan, he felt himself responsible for her. But what could he do about his heart, which was totally enamoured with Taji?

Lately, he could not even imagine a moment without her. She had overpowered not only his heart and mind but his senses too. What else could he do? Taji was so attractive that all who set eyes on her fresh, fulsome youth and rosy complexion found it hard to resist her spell.

Hameedan thought she held Shera securely within the strong fortress of her love and security. She never knew that one day a burning arrow shot from some unknown direction would so pierce the citadel that within a moment all would turn to ashes and ruin would stare her in the face.

Shera lifted the sackcloth curtain and entered the house. As usual, Hameedan was sitting before the fireplace on the right side of the courtyard cooking food. Just as on every other day, while she blew through the blower on to the smouldering cow-dung cakes and firewood, her big silver earrings shook, smoke billowed and her eyes watered. Even after so many years, Hameedan still hadn't learnt to kindle a fire properly. *Ammah* thought she was slack and lazy as it wasn't such a difficult task for womenfolk. It was really quite simple.

Ammah was in the habit of taunting Hameedan without rhyme or reason. She let pass no opportunity of complaining about her. Actually, Hameedan had not been her choice, but her son Shera's. When he had brought his bride home she had had to unwillingly accept her. But the real sorrow that was festering inside her was the fact that Hameedan was still barren. This was no small crime for *Ammah* to overlook. All day long she would keep reproaching Hameedan for her slowness in producing a grandchild.

Even the circumstances in which Shera had come to marry Hameedan gave his mother little joy.

"Wrath of God! What has an unmarried, good-looking young man got in common with a widow, who's given birth to a still-born baby after her husband died?'

It had seemed as if Shera had lost his senses. With no thought for the consequences he had stubbornly stated that he would either marry Hameedan or remain a bachelor all his life.

Hearing the slight noise, Hameedan raised her head. Her earrings swung wildly, wrapping themselves around her neck.

"You're back, Shera!" she smiled.

"Is dinner ready?" he asked as usual and went to wash his hands and face.

Hameedan quickly started making fresh *roti* for him. Silently Shera began eating his meal, while Hameedan felt happy just looking at him eat. "But why is he so quiet these days?" she thought. In the old days, sitting next to her he could not stop talking for a single moment: events of the day, his work in the fields, funny incidents – he would tell her everything. Then, he had not been able to decide which was more intoxicating, the aroma of freshly cooked *roti* or the scent emanating from Hameedan's body – which he could feel close by. To make his food go down more quickly, he would start gulping down water.

When Hameedan rubbed her eyes, which were red-rimmed from the smoke rising up from the logs, he would ask her tenderly, "Does the smoke irritate my *rani?*"

"Yes it does, it's very irritating," she would pout.

"Your eyes are really so lovely! As beautiful as ripe, golden wheat." He would praise her brown, almond-shaped eyes. "I swear upon God, I could spend my days and nights just looking at your eyes. They remain in my thoughts all day long. Just by looking at them I know what hour of the day it is!"

"What nonsense!" she would laugh.

"Really, Hameedan, you don't know what magic you have in your eyes! At dawn, the golden sun of hope for a fine day rises in them and as the day goes by, they shine with a message of contentment and peace."

He would burst out laughing at her serious expression. "Oh, you're so silly. If you had gone to school you would've known what I'm talking about." He would boast about his superiority as he had gained matriculation.

Shera was her whole life: he had loved her so much she thought she could never be proud enough of her good fortune. But sometimes he would say to her, "Look Hameedan, I hope you'll always keep my love," and she would grow afraid.

Besides loving Shera, she felt grateful to him for having married her. Before that, she had quietly accepted a barren life as her destiny. Her life had been useless, purposeless – an arid desert. She had been offered no respect or value by her in-laws, but she was constrained to live with them since she had no close relatives other than her parents, who had long been dead.

Three years after the death of her husband, languishing in her in-laws' house, she had turned into a lifeless, rough lump of wood. Watching life pass her by through her big, soulless eyes, she wondered why it refused to stay a while and cast a glance at her as well.

She had donned the cloak of darkness and the clogs of renunciation. But one day a new morning knocked at her door and startled her. The name of the sun on that glorious morning was Shera. The lustre of that sun dazzled her. Sudden light spread all around and Hameedan's eyes were filled with radiance. Hameedan was not even fully aware when she ornamented her palms with this golden sun and, spreading its glitter over her face, climbed into the silver chariot.

Shera too remembered well the day that he had first caught sight of Hameedan at his friend Afzal's house. She was Afzal's sister-in-law. Everybody knew about her but no one realized that somewhere within the fragile, sorrowful stem of this pale rose lay a longing for life. When Shera set eyes on this delicate, melancholy girl in her early twenties, he found himself helplessly hypnotized by her big brown eyes. He started visiting Afzal's house on one pretext or another and grew familiar with every member of the family. Sometimes Hameedan brought in the tea and sometimes food, and, lost in thought, Shera would keep on staring at her. It mattered not to him that Hameedan was a ravaged woman who had passed through storms nor what her social status was. He was aware only of one thing, that he felt drawn to her. Gradually their eyes started communicating with each other and reluctantly Hameedan gave herself up to silky, colourful dreams.

After a great deal of thought Shera asked *Ammah* to make a formal proposal to Hameedan's in-laws for his marriage to her. *Ammah*, as expected, raised hell. It had never even crossed her mind that her unmarried only son might have fallen head over heels in love with a widow – and mother of a still-born baby at that!

"That hag must've cast a spell over you. I know all about the machinations of these women. May the wrath of God fall on her! Isn't she content even after gobbling up her husband and child? That vampire has now fixed her eyes on my home. I'll never send a proposal for her!"

Ammah beat her chest and started wailing. The neighbours soon got to know about it as did the relatives. It spread like a whirlwind and the news rapidly reached Hameedan's in-laws.

"My daughter-in-law! What about the prestige of my family! Someone linked with my dead son's name, to be remarried! How's that possible?" Her father-in-law roared and her mother-in-law uttered such dire threats to break her legs and shut her up indoors that Hameedan found it difficult to breathe, and turned back once again into the weak stem of a pale rose.

The tiny, coloured dreams which had become her companions she placed inside the great, iron trunk of helplessness, turned the lock of caution and poured the ashes of loneliness in her hair. Swords were drawn by relatives on either side. Curses and abuses rained down and mud was slung.

Shera may have lost hope but it was impossible for him to forget Hameedan.

One evening his friend Achoo *Pehlawan*, finding him sad and worried, asked the reason why. Shera told him everything, adding that he could not even imagine life without Hameedan. Achoo had a fit of laughter when he heard this. He was so rolling about with mirth that he knocked the bottle of oil from the hand of the young lad massaging him.

"Oh, what a stuffed lion you are! You have become a lover but you haven't yet learnt to become a real lion! I can't see any problem in what you've just told me."

"But what, my friend, can I do? *Ammah* is not ready to agree! And now on top of it all Hameedan's in-laws are also on the warpath! I can't think what to do!"

"What does it matter, my friend! Why are you so scared? When will you stop sitting around wearing bangles like a woman? After all you're a man! Act like one – carry her off and marry her

– bring her here to my place. I'll get her married to you right here – if Achoo *Pehlawan* is with you, who'd dare stop you? Don't you worry about that!"

With Achoo's encouragement, Shera found new strength of heart. Really, it wasn't all that difficult after all! Nor was it so very unlikely!

He began looking for the right chance. One morning while it was still dark, he saw Hameedan walking sedately to the fields with her sisters-in-law. Shera galloped towards them and suddenly whisked up his bride. The other girls' screams could be heard far away in all directions. Hameedan's heart-beats gained speed but were lost in the sound of the horse's galloping hooves.

Achoo *Pehlawan* quickly arranged for the *maulvi* and witnesses. Hameedan could hardly grasp a thing. Perhaps it was a dream. But no dream had ever proved to be so sweet. She nodded her assent with eyes tightly shut and only heard the clamour of congratulations. She feared that if she opened her eyes the beads of this wonderful dream-necklace would break and scatter and she would be left empty-handed.

The news of their marriage caused the relatives' swords to be drawn once again and hostilities resurfaced but it was too late, nothing could be done now. Under the circumstances no one could say a word and the incident was soon forgotten.

Hameedan, after becoming Shera's wife, would hop around proudly like a chirpy sparrow. She learnt to laugh and entertain once again and, wearing the paddy-green wrap of Shera's love over her head, she felt herself protected from all sorrows, anxieties, fears and apprehensions. Being the passionate love of a man as fearless as Shera transformed the weak Hameedan into a strong woman. She had no fear of the world now, nor did she take her mother-in-law's jibes to heart. She had so much pride in the love of her man that this confidence gave her a new sparkle. She swung about like polished, silver earrings. Other girls were envious of her good fortune.

Time passed.

And with the passing of time Hameedan's love for Shera grew greater day by day. Shera's passion, however, grew still like calm waters. One likely reason for the calmness was that the tiny hand, that could make waves on its glassy surface by throwing pebbles, lived somewhere far away. Nobody knew which land he inhabited, nor why he failed to shed his beams on their courtyard. Five years had passed. Hameedan became lost in gloom while Shera ignored the subject. But *Ammah* had no need to keep quiet. All day long she heaved sighs, made biting remarks and wounded Hameedan's heart, but Hameedan said not a word in her own defence. When *Ammah* urged, she would visit *hakeems,* seers and tombs of saints but perhaps God did not will it and so their yearnings remained unfulfilled.

Now even the relatives and the neighbours had started raising fingers in gossip.

"Sardaran has a lot of patience. She has allowed a fruitless tree to take root in her courtyard. If Hameedan had been my daughter-in-law, I would've thrown her out by now."

"Didn't I say she'd turn out to be unlucky! First, she's a widow, secondly, she gave birth to a dead child and now on top of it all she hasn't even produced an heir. Yet look at the way she stomps around! The cheek of it! She's not modest or shameful."

"I wonder if there's something wrong with her or she wouldn't have had a dead baby."

Although rebuked from every side, she seemed not to mind. Shera was her sanctuary, his love was her strength, the secret of whose hidden presence was known only to her.

As long as Samson had his locks of hair, he could not be overpowered. But one day he fell asleep. Quietly Delilah crept close to him and cruelly cut those tresses which gave him strength. He became weak and helpless.

That day, running off after stealing sugar cane from the cane fields, Taji collided so hard with Shera that all his control, principles, morals and fidelity came crashing down to the ground. Lightning flashed and the warmth of a new, youthful, virgin's touch burnt Shera down in a minute.

That day for the first time he found Hameedan's bosom cold, stale and time-worn and he felt scared. How had this transformation came about? It was beyond his comprehension. Anxiously he wondered, "I thought I had reached my goal but what is this new goal that Taji has offered me!"

Like a golden stalk of sugar cane, Taji was hard on the outside but luscious within. Shera could not help but touch this sugar cane and his hands grew sticky. Placing his lips on the succulent cane, he felt its fresh sweetness entering his blood. What was this fiery sweetness that made Shera powerless? He abandoned himself to its flames. He had no command over himself as he set off to see Taji. He found her waiting for him in the cane field but she would not let him quench his thirst. The more he tasted her sweetness, the more his desire increased.

When he returned home, Hameedan, blowing on the firewood and cow-dung cakes, seemed like a stranger. Her eyes, burning with the effort of making fire, no longer offered him their former warmth. He would quickly eat his meal and lie down indoors. Turning from side to side he would imagine Taji next to him by his side and, closing his eyes, he would pretend to be asleep.

The sugar cane field enthralled him. He had started coming home late. When rumours spread in the village, they reached *Ammah* as well. Taji was no coward like Hameedan. She would proudly run around telling her friends about her rendezvous with Shera.

When *Ammah* asked Shera what was going on, he quietly looked away, but from his eyes she recognized hidden new love and the desire to keep it. What possible objection could *Ammah* have? Hope once again flickered in her heart. The expectation of playing with a tiny, rosy grandson, of a gorgeous, glittering dowry, of a new virgin daughter-in-law brought lustre to her old eyes and she thought: last time, Shera insisted on pushing himself clumsily into marriage but this time I'll garland my son myself for the ceremony, invite the whole clan to the feast; I'll wear a red dress and dance with the other women. I'll have everything I wanted.

But first something had to be done about Hameedan. Both mother and son brooded day and night on the problem of Hameedan.

Gradually Taji also started frequenting their house on one pretext or another, and grew quite intimate with *Ammah*.

"Allow me to massage your head with oil, *Khala*. Look how dry it is!"

"Let me pick out the gravel from the pulses for you, Hameedan *Apa*!"

"May I starch Shera's turban for him? Give fodder to his horse? Hang up his waistcoat on the hook?"

In the beginning Hameedan didn't find anything objectionable in Taji's increasing visits to their house, but when gradually she noticed Shera's growing attentiveness to Taji she was afflicted with grief. Never in her wildest dreams had she imagined that Delilah would have already left with Samson's hair, and his statue, fallen from its pedestal, would lie broken in pieces.

"This common woman won't enter this house again!" she shouted to prove her authority as owner of the house and Shera's wife.

"Well, she's my relative! Why shouldn't she come to visit me!" *Ammah* said stubbornly. Taji was indeed a distant relative and *Ammah* used this reference to defend her.

"Why should she come? Are you planning to give her my place? Remember, *Ammah*, you'll never manage that so long as I'm alive. I won't put up with it!" she raged like a tigress.

"Shera, why don't you tell her that I can bring whatever bride I choose for my son. I'll only get a grandson if I get another daughter-in-law."

Ammah put all her cards on the table. Without so much as a glance at Hameedan, Shera picked up his turban and left the house. Feeling deeply nervous, he was hurrying towards the sugar cane field when he met Taji on the way.

"Whatever's the matter? Why are you so pale? And why are you sweating?"

Taji wiped the beads of sweat from Shera's forehead with her wrap. Both of them sat in the shade of a huge banyan tree. It was growing dark and tired birds were flying back to their nests. Exhausted, Shera leaned his head on Taji's shoulder and she stroked him gently.

"That witch must have said something! Why don't you tell her everything?" Taji said frowningly.

"I did tell her but she said she would never allow it. Look, Taji, I can't throw her out of the house. What can I do? I'm at my wits' end!"

The bird looked towards its nest for help.

"Okay then! Stay with her – but then why are you dallying with me? If you had truly loved me, you wouldn't have kept me away, you would've married me and taken me into your home. I never knew you were such a coward. Can't you do it for the sake of our love? It must be true then that all men are equally selfish!"

Her eyes filled with tears, she removed Shera's head from her shoulder and, sobbing wildly, she walked off. Shera watched as she went further and further away.

Taji, his life, his soul, was leaving displeased, and he was incapable of doing a thing. His heart sank and, with feeble steps, he walked down the lane.

"Hameedan!" he roared like a lion as he entered the house, "I'm going to marry Taji and no power on earth can stop me!" Shera picked up a log and stoked it in the fire, angrily.

"But . . . but . . . you love only me. You are mine!" Words stuck in her throat.

"I did love you once, but now I love her! Can't you understand this much? Am I kicking you out of the house? You can stay here too but just don't thrust yourself at me. I didn't promise to be tied to you for the whole of my life! And you want me to do just that!"

Shocked, Hameedan stared at him and wondered if promises written with life-breath and heart-beats carried any value. Are promises only those which are written in black and white?

She was lost in thought and would have gone on sitting like that for a good deal longer if she hadn't been startled out of her reverie by the pot boiling over.

"Take more care when you cook. Do you want to starve me to death today?" Grumbling, Shera placed the turban on his head and walked out. Unable to sort out his problems, he wasn't even aware of where he was going, but his feet unconsciously carried him to the wrestling arena of Achoo *Pehlawan.*

"What's the matter, pal? Why such a long face?" his friend asked affectionately, and Shera could not hold back: out it all came.

Achoo laughed heartily. "Really, you're a lion in name only. A friend of Achoo *Pehlawan,* and helpless on account of a mere female? Is that something to get worked up over? If you're weary of one female, get yourself another one! For heaven's sake, don't be such a wimp. Do whatever you want, be like a real man. And be brave – I'll stand by you!"

Patting Shera on the back he gave him new determination and strength.

Hameedan's world was collapsing around her. Once again she sought treatment for fertility. She got to hear that a new *peer* had arrived in a neighbouring village. The fame of his miracles had spread far and wide. It was said that he could help anyone who came.

Somehow or other Hameedan reached his abode and begged for fecundity. The *peer* listened to her attentively and prayed to God especially for her. He gave her two amulets and instructed her to pray regularly.

Tiny lamps of hope flickered in the darkness of Hameedan's heart. She followed the *peer*'s instructions carefully, hanging one amulet around her neck and the other one on a branch of the tree in the courtyard. Days flew by. Shera and *Ammah* communicated only through their eyes and said nothing before Hameedan. As Taji no longer came to their house any more, Hameedan was lulled into believing that she had broken it off with Shera.

"Good riddance!" Hameedan sent a silent prayer of thanks to God and once more busied herself in the service of Shera and *Ammah*.

Ammah went away for a few weeks to visit her brother in his village. It was her custom to go and see her brothers and sisters from time to time. After she left, Shera grew more grave and was mostly lost in thought.

Hameedan wished that things at home would once again improve and she mulled it over constantly. One day her body gave her the glad tidings. This was the news for which she had yearned. She couldn't believe that at last a flower was blooming within her body. Eagerly, she hurried to her distant aunt for confirmation. Her aunt enquired closely about her condition and, satisfied, congratulated her. Quickly an offering of one and a quarter rupees was sent to the mosque. She found the walk back hard going. She wished that she could slowly reach home floating on air. She didn't dare go too fast in case she harmed the bud growing within her. She became anxious. "Will I be able to look after the baby? It will be so tiny, so fragile! What would I do?"

Lost in thought she walked home. Numerous sparrows sitting in the green field of wheat, seeing her pass close by, sang congratulations in her ear and flew away.

"Naughty birds!" she scolded them, lovingly.

"Hurry home!" the golden wheat, which resembled her own eyes, seemed to say.

"Now Shera won't have to find a new woman!" a gust of breeze whispered in her ear. Hameedan swung along happily.

In the evening, Shera entered the house as usual and was amazed to find it utterly transformed. Everything looked neat, clean and new. A clean tablecloth on the table, immaculate bedsheets, freshly mud-plastered courtyard. Instead of the dirty plastic flowers in the vase, there were fresh roses. *Ammah* wasn't at home so there was no chatter from her. Yet the house did not seem empty or desolate but was filled with Hameedan's presence. On the crocheted shelf-cover lay the tape-recorder, on which Shera's favourite Punjabi songs were being played. Uncomprehendingly Shera looked at Hameedan and could not take his eyes off her. There was a strange bloom about her. She was wearing her red bridal dress and all her gold ornaments which she had not worn of late. The gold ornaments looked so beautiful on her they seemed to have a special glow. This evening, as usual she was sitting on the low stool cooking dinner. The courtyard was scented with the aroma of spices and fresh *roti*.

Hearing the rattle of the door opening, instead of looking up towards Shera, Hameedan began blowing hard on the kindling. She didn't even seem to mind the tears running down her cheeks.

"Hameedan." Shera called softly.

Hameedan turned round to look at him. When the curtain of her eyelashes rose, Shera saw the luminous eyes filled with a world of longing and love. Such dreamy kohl had never adorned those eyes before. Such colours of sunset had never beautified her cheeks before. Such redness had never earlier become the fate of that rosebud mouth. Shera came close and sat beside her. Feeling the warmth of his presence, Hameedan blushed and her body started trembling.

"You've been spoiling your lovely eyes in this acrid smoke for so many years now. When you entered the house after our marriage, they were like full-blown roses. Now they are ruined, always red-rimmed."

He lovingly touched the lock of hair that had fallen forward on Hameedan's face. From who knew where, the ocean entered Hameedan's eyes and everything was washed out.

"Shera!" Overcome with emotion, Hameedan sobbed convulsively while she clutched at Shera's arm. Her body was trembling weakly. She so wanted to tell him the good news quickly, that their world would soon be complete. "The flower of creation is waiting to blossom forth," she wanted to say, but couldn't find the right words.

"Come on – up you get! You're crazy to start crying just now. Come out and see what I've brought for you! But you have to close your eyes first!"

Leaving Hameedan in a dazed state, he carried in something from outside. Then he asked her to open her eyes.

"Whatever is that?" Hameedan looked in astonishment at the thing that Shera was setting down, draped with a piece of cloth.

"What's this you've brought?" she exclaimed. Shera revealed an oil-stove.

"From now on, you can cook on this," he said. "Look! No firewood, no dung-cakes, no blower or smoke and no spoiling your eyes."

"Oh, thank you! But Shera, you needn't have done this! I've never complained. You shouldn't have gone to all this trouble!"

"It was no trouble at all! Can't I even do this much for my Hameedan! Look, it's so easy to use. Let me show you. You must make me an egg pudding on this stove, right now, today. I haven't had one for ages! I'd really love some today!"

Shera got up and patted the oil-stove from all sides. He checked the oil in the tank. It was filled to the brim. Then he pulled up the brand-new cotton wicks so they were half in the oil and half out. After fully satisfying himself that the stage was all set for the fireworks, he got up, stretching himself.

"I'll go and get changed. In the meantime, all you do is strike a match and ignite it here, like this." He gave the instructions to her and got up. Hameedan picked up the matchbox.

Before going into the room, Shera stopped to make sure that the door leading out of the courtyard was locked securely – so that no one could get out through there either.

Originally translated from the Urdu
by Atiya Shah

Tumbleweed

Azra Asghar

Where she's gone, nobody knows. Probably to her empty hostel room or maybe somewhere else. For a long while I've just been sitting on the revolving chair by my desk, lost in jumbled thoughts. I've picked up the paperweight from the desk and started turning it on its smooth side. Small, brightly coloured flowers are imprisoned exquisitely inside the paperweight; I don't know how. But I do know this much at least, that a little while back, she was sitting here, on the other side of the desk, facing me, and filling up her admission form. Flora, with pale complexion and snub nose. She handed me the form and gazed at me. I took no notice of her fixed look and kept my eyes on her form, although I knew that her bright, narrow eyes were watching me closely. I am used to this and realize that students try to gauge their own competence and ability from the teacher's expression, just as an infant's mother understands her child's needs and knows what's making it cry. Students too try to read in the changing facial expressions of their teacher whether they are considered bright or dim. With this particular form the problem was not of competence or incompetence; so what, then, was she looking for in my face? What was she searching for? I skimmed over the form and handed it back saying:

"You haven't written in your father's name. Perhaps you forgot to write it." Her eyes fell from my face and with trembling hands she took back the form.

"Please fill in your father's name," I said politely. Habitually, we men while talking to ladies become gentle, courteous and very good-humoured. And in my profession I have to make sure I am patient and dignified at all times. I've been like this for so many years it has become second nature to me. Besides, the guiding hand that raised me was like the fire which transforms base metal into gold. Alas! the same benefactor, in his dying moments, dealt me a wound so deep that it may not heal even on my death . . .

"Son, now that I'm leaving this world, I think I should tell you that in reality you are not my true-born child. It was indeed I who, without a doubt, raised you, but I was not the one responsible for bringing you into this world."

"What do you mean, Papa!" I asked in confusion, taking hold of his cold, trembling hand.

"I'm telling you the truth, my son. Listen to me carefully. I might never have divulged it to you but this world is very cruel. Maybe after my death, you'd have found out the truth and considered me guilty. So, I think the time has come to tell you everything that has been kept a secret until now. It all happened when my career was just beginning. I was the Head of a big school. I loved a certain girl and planned to marry her soon. Then one day a beautiful young girl, holding a three- or four-year-old child by the hand entered my office . . ."

"May I help you?" I asked politely.
"Sir, this is my child," she said in a refined accent.
"Yes, I can see that, a sweet child!"
"Please admit him to your school."
"Certainly, just fill up this form," I said, giving her the form.
"Have you room for him in the hostel?" she asked.

"I'm sorry, we have no arrangements for such small children."

"Then that will be a problem." She became lost in thought.

"Don't you live here?"

"No." She looked me straight in the eye.

"Well, fill out the form anyway. We'll think about arrangements for boarding later on." I don't know what prompted me to say that. She filled up the form. In the column for the father's name she wrote her own name.

"What's this?" I said pointing at it.

"Sir, I am both his father and mother." Her boldness in speaking impressed me deeply.

"Do you mean to say . . ."

"No, no, Sir, he is my legitimate son." She understood what I meant.

"His father has divorced me and I don't even want that man's shadow to fall upon me or my son. He exploited us cruelly. Even on the Day of Judgement everyone is recognized by the name of the mother. If God is so merciful to mankind and holds our trust, why then may we not associate our children with our own names?"

"You're right, Madam, but it is also God's law that in this world we are recognized by the name of the father. If it weren't so, immorality would become the order of the day."

"But I'll never allow the name of that man to be given to my son. He shunned us and turned us out into the darkness of night."

"All the same, in education, the rules do not allow for your wishes."

"Then write in your own name," she said spontaneously, and I have no idea what it was that prompted me to write my own name – Ali Ahmad Syed – in that empty space.

"Very well then, young Shujaat will stay with me from now on." I got up from my chair, picked you up and seated you next to me.

"Sir, I'll never forget what I owe you. I shall worry no more. Whatever happens I can live anywhere now. I shall have no regrets even if I die." Tears rolled from your mother's eyes which I dried with my words of consolation. After that your mother came a few times to visit you and then she went abroad. She was a great woman and you may well imagine she's dead. But she's not, she's still alive and her address is written in my diary. You can confirm the truth of this story from the lady whom I desired to marry, but could not because of my responsibility for your upbringing. I wanted you to study hard and become a great man. Thank God, I achieved my aim. Now I can die in peace."

Papa did not survive long after this and soon left me alone in this world. I took up his profession, as my great love for him could find solace only in teaching. I taught not schoolchildren but foreign students, who came to study Urdu with me. I am now a professor at a big college.

"Excuse me, Sir, can't I write something else instead of my father's name?"

"What else, for example – and why?" I don't know what thoughts filled my mind when I said this involuntarily, looking at her pale face. Her eyes were still fixed on the form and, holding the pen in the air, she sat silent. Her face grew even paler.

"Sir, I come from Vietnam," she said sorrowfully.

"I know."

"Our country has been at war for many years now."

"I'm aware of that too."

"We were victims of savagery by foreigners in our country."

"So I believe."

"Then, Sir, surely you also know that Vietnam is full of children like me. We are those unfortunate children who never knew our fathers." Tears rolled from her lustrous, narrow eyes and blotted the form, over which she was bent. I took the pen gently from her hand, pulled the form towards me and wrote, Flora, daughter of Shujaat Ali Ahmad.

"Sir— ?" Her eyes widened in surprise.

"Yes, child, this is my name. Our books of wisdom tell us that a teacher is like a father, and if that is the case, you are my daughter."

A string of teardrops ran down her pale cheeks. I consoled her, saying, "This is not your problem alone. It is the tragedy of all civilized, developed nations who, in the name of progress, teach small nations how to stay alive and then seize their very lives. They give them grain, then snatch away the morsel that reaches their mouths. They give them weapons for protection and then kill them with those same weapons. They teach them the meaning of liberty but control their right to live. Once, a foreign power entered United India in triumph, and then departed, leaving behind a horde of 'tommy' children. This is not just your own tragedy, Flora, this is the tragedy of every slave nation. Every victorious nation makes the nation it defeats a victim of barbaric cruelty. And what is more, Flora, in every country woman is held in low esteem and as long as woman is considered so low, she will continue to be the target of man's brutality. Be strong, Flora, be strong! You are the daughter of a strong Vietnamese mother. Courage and strength were bestowed on you by your mother's milk. Be brave and break these chains of slavery which bind you in the name of culture."

She is gone. Lost in chaotic thoughts, I toy with the paperweight. Small, brightly coloured flowers are skilfully, exquisitely imprisoned within, and I, seated in my revolving chair, am lost in confused reflection. This world may no doubt be like a revolving chair – a full turn may take many years – yet nothing stops it spinning on.

Those upon it may indeed suffer change, but it remains ineluctably the same.

Originally translated from the Urdu
by Atiya Shah

Paper Money
Razia Fasih Ahmed

Superstition in the twentieth century is by no means in decline. I discovered this when I first went to see the house in which I now live. It is small but beautiful, with two bedrooms, a lovely kitchen and a nice garden – not a common feature in city houses these days. It immediately caught my fancy and I took it on the spot. The rent was fairly low. The owner told me the place had been empty a long time. It was surprising that such a nice house remained vacant in Karachi for over a year. When the neighbours told me it was haunted, I was not in the least perturbed. Somehow it just accounted for the low rent.

Being a writer and an educated man, I am not at all superstitious. As soon as the house was cleaned up and repainted, I moved in. I had it redecorated in a simple style, to suit my own taste. What I liked best about the house was the long, narrow room on the upper level which had huge windows opening on to the garden. There was a pine tree nearby – a rare thing in Karachi. The long green branches of this pine tree tapped against the window panes on windy nights. The moon looked beautiful peeping through the branches into my room. It somehow made me happy. I called this room my study and felt that being there helped me organize my thoughts better. I could always write well in this room.

Temperamentally I am an introvert, and my profession makes me even more so. My neighbours were kind enough to call on me and considered it their duty to warn me about the house. The legend had it that the ghost in the house went for the owner's most precious possession. Thus, one family had lost a son, another a daughter, still another all its wealth, and the last man who inhabited the house had lost his mind. I told them, half jokingly, that I had neither a family nor wealth, nor was I a narcissist. I hardly possessed a single thing of value. My whole wealth consisted of my own books or books written by others, all of which were fortunately published in quite large numbers, so could easily be replaced if they happened to get lost.

They were disappointed by my attitude. After that we only met by chance in the street, where we would exchange greetings. Once in a while, however, especially around festival times, we called on each other at home.

I used to cook my own food, but had a woman sweeper to clean the house. Her name was Shanti. Shanti means "peace" in Hindi. She was very calm and quiet, but dull-witted. In the beginning I tried to order her about, but either she did not understand what I said or pretended she didn't, so I soon gave up. She worked for me at half the rate that other sweepers charged. Somehow, without exchanging a word, we came to an agreement that she would work in her own way and I would not interfere. She never stole a thing; on the contrary she often found my pen or watch for me, possessions which I was in the habit of leaving in odd places.

Shanti was so dim she could not even count the money I gave her. Her husband had to come on the first of the month to collect her wages. He was very feeble and sickly and looked little wiser than his wife. I gradually lost all enthusiasm for talking to him because he seemed incapable of giving me a proper answer. But I must admit I often thought about them both. It is said that there is a law of compensation in nature. If a person lacks one thing he is endowed with another, but as far as I could tell, this couple had nothing. They were both old and ugly. They were both poor and stupid, and only had each other. I often thought of writing a short story about them but for some reason could not.

Once when I was thinking about writing a new novel, I chanced to read *The Story of a Novel* by Thomas Wolfe. He performed a unique experiment in novel-writing by first jotting down all his thoughts about the details and then shaping them into a novel. He himself wrote: "There was nothing at first which could be called a novel. I wrote about night and darkness in America, and the faces of the sleepers in ten thousand little towns, and of the tides of sleep and how the rivers flowed forever in the darkness. I wrote about death and sleep . . . I wrote about October, of great trains that thundered through the night, of ships and stations in the morning, of men in harbours and the traffic of the ships . . ." *October Fair* ended up about twelve times the length of *War and Peace* and it occurred to me that I might have a go at this technique of writing myself.

I started almost immediately and enjoyed recollecting and writing things without having to bother about fitting them into a plot. The result was almost the same as Wolfe's: a large bulk of papers that increased day by day. It took me two years to assemble my ideas until one day I realized that I could not keep on in this way and now had to start giving it some shape. That was the most tedious and difficult job – turning this great bulk into a book. However, I was in the middle of doing it, and was starting to enjoy it thoroughly, when suddenly the manuscript disappeared.

I searched every nook and cranny but could not find it anywhere. I asked Shanti about it but she was as innocent as a child. She seemed hardly to understand what I was talking about and so I soon gave up. It was then that the idea of the house being haunted came to my mind. The manuscript was the most precious thing I had at that time. Yes, there was no doubt it was precious to me. For anyone else, it might just have been a bundle of papers, but for me it meant everything – my whole life. I knew I would never be able to write those things in the same way again. I have found that once I transfer a memory on to paper it either disappears completely or so fades away that I am unable to reproduce it again as fully as before.

I tried my best to recall whether I had lost anything else over these past years, but I could not remember a single item – apart from the odd book or magazine, which I am rather careless about. I always leave them lying around or pass them on to others who want to read them.

I was really upset about losing the fruits of my hard labour over not just months, but years; I felt miserable, as if some calamity had befallen me. I lost my appetite as I was constantly racking my memory trying to think where on earth my beloved manuscript might be. That manuscript haunted me. I saw it in my dreams; I experienced strange illusions about it. I often thought I saw it on my writing-table but when I drew near it was gone. Sometimes I felt certain I would find it in one of my drawers and I would open them one by one as if some miracle was about to occur but alas there would be nothing there. No miracle. The manuscript had been spirited away without a trace.

When I told my neighbours about the disappearance of my manuscript, they were certain I must have done something to annoy the ghost, which, in revenge, had taken the most precious thing I happened to possess at the time. One of the neighbours brought a seer with him, who was meant to be able to tell where the manuscript was. The seer wrote something on numerous pieces of paper, put them all in an earthenware pot and asked me to hold on to its rim with my index finger. He supported the pot with his own index finger placed on the other side. He recited something and the pot started moving. Then, after taking out all the pieces of paper, he started putting them back in the pot one by one while reciting his *mantra*. When one particular slip of paper went in, the pot moved again. He removed the paper and told me that my manuscript was still on the premises and I was likely to find it in a week's time. I paid no attention to what he said as it seemed just like a game. But I gave him money all the same and he and my neighbour went away happy, assuming that I had been deeply impressed by the seer.

Worn out from mental anguish, sleeplessness and hunger, I wandered around like a ghost myself. I felt dejected and frustrated with nothing to do. I felt as though my whole fortune had gone. Still in this miserable state of mind, I one day came across Shanti's husband rummaging through the garbage in the back lane. He was sorting out the used cans, empty cigarette packets, dirty rags and torn pieces of paper. He even had a pile of putrefied fruit and vegetables in front of him. I asked him what he was going to do with all that rubbish. He said he was going to take the vegetables and fruit home and the rest he would sell for five *paise*. I was shocked to hear that. I had no idea that the poverty of my fellow countrymen had reached such a low level. Shanti and her husband were collecting all this rubbish to sell for practically nothing. Stung by shame, I decided to increase Shanti's salary.

I returned home, completely exhausted. Stepping across my lawn I noticed something half hidden in the banana grove. Though very upset and depressed, I could still be driven by curiosity. I went closer to see what it could be. There were four sacks brim full of rubbish, which Shanti and her husband had been collecting, perhaps for weeks. I again felt a pang of pain and shame. All this they would sell to raise enough for a day's meal, perhaps. All of a sudden, a strange thought came into my mind. I madly emptied out the contents of the sack and there to my surprise was the manuscript of my novel – not in one of the sacks but in all four of them, torn into small pieces and smeared with all sorts of refuse. There too were pieces of the letters, magazines and books that I often found were missing but gave little thought to at the time.

Such was the helplessness of Shanti and her husband that they didn't even steal anything of value. They only stole papers on which something was written, for they thought these were as useless as empty tins, and tore them up to render them still more useless so that nobody could ever suspect them of stealing.

The manuscript for which I was hoping to get a lot of money had no value for them as it was, but transformed into a torn and dirty pack of paper it meant money to them. And this is how it happened that the manuscript which was going to be the greatest book of the century got lost forever.

Originally translated from the Urdu
by the author

Millipede
Khalida Hussain

I opened the door. After the dark, dank chill of inside, the assault of the outside glare and heat was quite unsettling. The springs faintly squeaked as the grey door with its dusty screen closed shut. Behind the door in the room, permeated by cloying odours of iodine and rubbing alcohol, people sat on leather-upholstered benches and faded chairs, listlessly flipping through the pages of *Mirror, Nawa-e-Waqt* and the *Pakistan Times*. Moments before I had been inside that room . . . and now outside . . . I was standing on the open porch, facing a small lawn fenced in by a dense citron hedge. From the porch I could only see a couple of flower beds, with their bright red roses and some tiny, cup-shaped yellow flowers, and a mud path that ran along the edge of the lawn and led up to a white wooden gate. I climbed down the five steps of the porch and followed the path to the gate. I opened the gate; its hinges also squeaked. The crowded street stretched out beyond.

As soon as I stepped out, I closed my eyes for a second, just to picture what I had seen. The reddish darkness slowly changed to green, and then a wavering stream of bright yellow spots, alternated with blackish-blue, then white. The outlines of things loomed up then grew dim. As the darkness twinkled, I felt again the familiar stifling lump in my throat. I gagged. My jaws began to go slack and my mouth fell wide open. I tried to grit my teeth.

My clenched fists began to throb with the effort but my teeth remained apart.

Finally, I took out the vial from my pocket and swallowed a pill. I knew that a millipede, a prehensile, myriapodal life was squirming inside me, slowly digging its slithery long limbs into me, driving them right into my veins. But I still couldn't believe it. Inside that room, the doctor, too, had said so. But I wondered how a worm could grow inside me! Absolutely impossible.

The pill dissolved in my mouth. My jaws slowly began to come together. I looked again at the crowded street ahead. People, motor-rickshaws, taxi-cabs, bicycles and scooters flowed in an unbroken stream. A man wearing thick, black-rimmed glasses stood in Hameed General Merchants store looking at the newspaper and casually running his free hand through his hair. Next to him a snub-nosed boy with thick black hair and slouching shoulders was laying out along the counter jar after jar of bright, colourfully labelled facial creams in a vivid display for the veiled woman. Shiny items of every colour were stacked up on the store's shelves.

Hameed General Merchants! I realized with surprise that although I had passed by here scores of times, I had never really noticed this store until today. Then came Salman Shoes, and then Amin Drug Store, followed by King's Barber Shop in which a young man in a barber's cloak was getting a head massage. The masseur's face was all red while the blue veins on his temples were so puffed up they seemed about to burst at any moment. On the radio, Zahida Parveen was singing a Sindhi *kafi*. I knew it was Zahida Parveen; I could easily tell her voice from other singers, even in a group or at a distance. But there are people – why, even friends of mine – who cannot distinguish one voice from another. That amazes me.

A scrawny man with a small boy in tow emerged from Salman Shoes. The boy held a shoe box tied with string, his tiny eyes all agleam. Then I realized that I had been walking in the wrong direction. I turned around and walked up to the motor-rickshaw stand. Three rickshaws stood side by side, two of them unattended, while in a third the driver was sprawled out in a leisurely way puffing at his cigarette.

On that day, for the first time, I noticed how magnificent rickshaws looked: I wasn't looking at a rickshaw at all, I was looking instead at some animate platform in motion which, I thought, would suddenly turn its head as it floated by and look at me and moan, just as that millipede squirming inside me would turn around to look at me and moan.

The driver took a long drag and looked me over, then asked unenthusiastically, "Where to, Sir?"

"Samnabad."

"Hop in," he said as he flipped the meter and started up the rickshaw. And then he broke into a popular film song, *Roke zamana chahe roke khuda'i.*

The seats inside were done up in bright vinyl with red and green floral patterns. A mirror was set into the iron lattice-work immediately behind the driver's seat. Coloured silk tassels swung all along the doorways on both sides of the cab.

The wind was quite hot and mixed with the odour of gasoline and dust, which reminded me, all of a sudden, that I was finally heading in the direction of Samnabad. What is Samnabad? No, Saman Abad – I tried to fix the pronunciation in my mind. I reeled at the thought – which was occurring to me, I believe, for the first time – that I was forgetting *names.* And things, when their names are lost, die. I didn't want to lose the names; so I tried to read every word on the billboards as they flew past me: Gehwara-e-Adab, Shaikh Ataullah Advocate, Butterfly Brand Nalki, Shabnam Garam Masalah, Love Potions – which will draw your cold-hearted girlfriend right to you . . . But then a whole lot of them by the side of the road and on the walls whirled by too fast for me to read. So I tried to repeat the names of the objects nearest to me. There were plenty of them in the rickshaw that I could identify by name; and then I had quite a few more inside, with me and on me: my shirt, tie, tie-pin, pen, wallet, bills, coins . . . but God knows how and why objects had become divorced from their names and here I was desperately trying to preserve those very names.

Since that moment I have made it my habit to repeat names of things to myself. In fact I am obsessed with the desire to behold the thing itself in its name. This is probably the reason why my mind is forever compiling a long inventory of names, as though I might some day find myself somewhere, where I might be asked to read it off.

This fixation with names has been growing day by day. Sometimes I feel jealous of people around me. My jealousy turns into burning hatred and envelops me like a dark madness when I realize that these people know names that I never will; these names will never become part of my memory. These people have stashed away those names inside themselves on purpose: it makes me hate them all the more.

This strange, irresistible fascination with names makes me feel as though I might manage to write something after all. In fact, I first became aware of my urge to write fifteen or twenty years ago. I even bought a sheaf of paper and set out all my writing materials neatly on the table. But the moment I picked up my pen, I felt that – no – I didn't want to write after all; instead, I wanted to read. It wasn't yet time to write. The right time would come some day. So I started to read. After I'd read a few lines I now felt I was ready to write. I again picked up my pen; again I couldn't write. Well, perhaps, there weren't yet words for the sort of things I wanted to write about. Yes, that must be it. I put down my pen and began to read again. After a while I knew that I didn't want to read after all. I stopped reading altogether . . . Fifteen or twenty years later – now – it was strange indeed that I'd all of a sudden felt not only that I wanted to write but that I *could* write. I bought myself a sheaf of paper and laid out my writing materials carefully on the table. I picked up the pen and wrote continuously for several hours until perspiration began to drip from my brow and the pen began to shake in my aching fingers. But all I had managed to write, I saw, were merely names, belonging to this thing or that. This, then, was really what I'd wanted to write all along: names of things – just that, the names of things I knew, had seen and keep on seeing.

If I could write down the names of all those things, it would certainly fill hundreds of pages. But when would I get a break from work to do that? Someone or other sticks close to me all day long checking up and giving me my medicine, no matter how often I've told everyone that I can take the medicine myself when it's time. I even have a watch with a third hand for the seconds! Yet they still hover round me the whole time and won't let me be.

I certainly have no wish to divulge the secret of my writing. And for a very good reason. Once, I made the barest allusion to one of my friends that continuous, coherent writing meant absolutely nothing: what a writer should do instead is collect names, I said, just names. Every person should search and gather up every name, indicating their essence, their reality. But that elicited only a good laugh from my friend. "Well, in that case," he replied, "dictionaries are the world's greatest literature."

His ignorance was depressing. Didn't he know dictionaries only had *words*, not *names*? Names, in fact, are the *very* things that exist with and within a man. And God forbid that man should come to forget the names of things that are his allotted share! Everyone should, therefore, preserve his identity, his things. But my friend, alas! He wouldn't understand any of this. So I kept my mouth shut.

I now work on my writing project in the evenings: unbeknown to anyone, quietly, secretly. But as soon as I put these names down on paper, I tend to forget them altogether. It's like this: the instant something comes out from within me, it dies. Am I, then, killing things off? Assiduously plucking them out of my flesh, blood and bones and tossing them away? How else could one hope to preserve anything? To find knowledge and keep it alive? Isn't it the case that we inevitably destroy a thing the instant we find it? This, perhaps, explains why so often at night just before falling asleep I consciously try to conjure up some forms before me and identify them by name. But the number of nameless things keeps increasing day by day, and I am sometimes obliged to refer back to the pages of my project halfway into the night. That invariably makes me despise even more the people living around me: they carry names in their bosoms, and yet appear indifferent to the tremendous responsibility imposed by this trust in them and appear to breathe with perfect ease, free of all care.

There are times, though, when I feel fed up with my writing project, mostly when I become suddenly aware of an infinite number of slithery appendages and stringy legs stirring deep inside me. Then I feel choked by the noose tightening around my jugular vein. My jaw goes slack and nauseating liquid wells up in my mouth, refusing to dribble out. And with that my mind goes mushy. I become convinced of the utter uselessness of my project – not just of the project, but of everything. Nothing and no name is more alive and more real than the wriggly millipede with its extended murderous claws.

My wife, though, quickly opens a vial and takes out a pill. "Take this. Quickly! Look, it's already half an hour late!"

I don't want the pill, but my voice changes as I speak, and sometimes it dies away altogether. At precisely such moments I remember the story about Dr Jekyll and Mr Hyde and feel the tremendous urge to witness the process of my own metamorphosis. But most of the time I stay away from mirrors. The truth is I don't have a single mirror in my room. For some time now a barber has been giving me a shave and when I comb my hair, looking in the mirror after my bath, I never manage to see the transmutation. Finally, one night, I stood a mirror nearby and went back to work on my writing project.

I feel there just aren't any more names to write. I've exhausted them all. Three or four names a day at best, I sit with pen in hand for hours, waiting. The names are finished. For I've poured them all out of my being; and when names are out, they no longer remain names, they change into words. That's why I feel totally empty, except, of course, in those moments when those scurrying, lively limbs wriggle and spread out inside me, sapping my vitality.

That night I sat with my pen ready. The clock was about to strike 1:30 – the time the alarm was set to go off. Every night my wife slept with the alarm set to ring every two hours so she could give me my medicine. But that night I reached out my hand and switched the alarm off. Slowly my jaw began to go slack and my eyelids began to droop. I clenched my fists as hard as I could and tried to bring my teeth together. The effort left me drenched with sweat. Suddenly, I could feel something wriggling in my throat and chest; the very worm that's growing inside me! It deftly sank its long pointed fangs into my jugular vein and a fluid darkness of pure comprehension surged over me. I quickly grabbed the mirror. As I looked into it, the ultimate uselessness of names hit me with unswerving certainty. I had lived with myself for all these years, always identifying myself with just a name. But this was superficial knowledge, deep inside which, like some kernel inside a hard shell, was another kind of knowledge as formless and nameless as the kernel itself. But that did have an identity. I looked incredulously at myself and felt something blow up in my temples with tremendous force.

"Oh – two o'clock already!" My wife sprang up from the bed, confused, then she brought a glass of water to my table. "Here," she said, "take this. Still up, then?"

"Yeah," I replied in a strangled voice. "Look, my jaw is going crooked!" I told her. She quickly turned her face away, pretending to wipe sweat off her brows with her *dupatta*. But I knew she was really wiping her tears away.

"No. You just didn't get your medicine on time. That's all. You'll be all right."

After that day I completely lost interest in my writing project. Everything was enclosed in a sheath inside which heaved a warm, live, slithery larva – a squiggly millipede. Everything concealed a spread-legged, vein-tugging myriapod in the lifeless cocoon of a name.

Consequently I have deleted most of the names from my memory and try to go through life with as few of them as possible. Often I cannot recall the names of the most essential objects. At such times my children just turn their faces away to wipe their tears, then turn back and carry on with cheerful, light-hearted gaiety.

Then, I tried to deal with the objects themselves – solid, tangible objects, shorn of the names signifying them. After all, what truly existed were the objects themselves, not their names. It was absolutely necessary to visualize them in their essence, without their accompanying names. I began to check on all the different things in the house. Sometimes while idly sitting, I would all at once find myself recalling an old, long-forgotten thing. For example, all of a sudden one night I thought of my old pipe. I jerked up from bed. It was absolutely imperative that I look at this *thing* – why, touch it. But God knows where it had been stashed away for all these years. I woke my wife up and tried to remind her of the pipe I used to smoke some six or seven years before, asking if she could think where it was.

"Go to sleep," my wife said, in a tearful voice. "Go back to sleep."

But I was persistent – and equally amazed at the tears that kept falling from her eyes. I got up and searched through the whole house for the pipe: trunks, cabinets, drawers, just about everything. At last I found it buried in the junk box. I looked at it, touched it and tossed it back in. I had satisfied myself of its existence. But, suppose it hadn't been there – what then? I couldn't bear to think about it. Gradually I stopped thinking about specific things. Now I'd look for whatever thing I could find. Things, countless things, no one thing in particular! One day my hands fell upon a bunch of yellow envelopes beneath a pile of rough paper, stumps of pencils and other odds and ends in a drawer. I recalled that these yellow envelopes contained the smooth grey X-ray negatives which had been taken a few months before. I held up the negatives to the light: a cage of curved ribs closing in upon a leech-like spine sprouting in the middle and filled with dark emptiness; the skull supported by the spinal column, reminding one of the label on bottles of toxic substances; and the prominent square mandible and pair of eye sockets spilling out dark, dank emptiness. On the lower corner of both the negatives was inscribed a name – *my name.*

Involuntarily I looked at my ribs and felt them, and my head covered with skin and hair. Then I looked at the bare, enclosing rib cage. Just then, that tactile myriapod began to spread out its countless legs and crawl about inside me, crushing my veins. I felt as though the millipede would suddenly turn its face towards me, stare at me and moan and that this would be nothing but the fluid darkness of pure meaning – inviolable, expanding, immortal, the first, the last, the sole essence of everything.

"Look! Look! This is really me!" I told my wife as I put the X-ray in front of her. She refused to understand a word.

"Yes," she said. "But these X-rays are no good any more. Just throw them out."

And at that very moment it hit me that it wasn't just me; that it was also my wife, my kids, my friends, my acquaintances – why, it was also all the people wandering in the cities, countryside and wilderness, that in the end the whole phenomenal world had absolutely no identity but for *the name* appearing in the bottom corners of those X-rays; that when a name comes out of a man, it dies.

But what is remarkable is that even after a name has died, the emptiness continues. Everything has its own unique emptiness – we all recognize the emptiness inside ourselves regardless of the way our eyes tell us that we apparently have no separate identity.

From this point on, therefore, my entire attention came to be riveted upon the millipede growing inside me. I wanted to know it, to see it. But the doctor says it couldn't be seen in any X-ray because it is a life – a growing, slithering, squirming, tactile life!

One day I was sitting with a bundle of papers before me. Each of the papers had countless names inscribed on it. But I failed to recognize even one of them. Suddenly that squirming life began to expand in me and I felt as though I was about to burst. Inside me something was gaining in size by the second, sucking every single vein and artery. I tried to draw breath. Sweat began to drip from my forehead. My wife quickly pried open my mouth and shoved one of those pills inside. But the place where my tongue should have been was filled with needles. The pill itself was a needle which joined the rest. Something was growing inside me . . . expanding . . . and my skin was about to burst. Then, instinctively, I knew the time for the anguished, piercing moan – that first and last word, that first and last sound – had finally come.

I heard the doctor say, "Get rid of this millipede! Come on, quickly, squash it!"

"No, no!" I wanted to say. "This carcinogenic, pulsating marrow, this slithering being has dominion over every part of my body, over every single pore – over every single *word* in the world!" So I wanted to say. But I don't remember what I actually did say . . . if I said anything at all. For by then my voice had died.

And now they are taking me away . . . I know they are taking me away . . . I know they are taking me away . . . I know they are taking me away . . . somewhere outside . . . to some old, desolate place . . . out in the dark, desolate wilderness . . . where they will squash my millipede . . . the first and the last sound . . . the first and the last word . . . in the dark, deep stillness . . .

Originally translated from the Urdu by
Muhammad Umar Memon and
Wayne R. Husted

The Spell and the Ever-Changing Moon

Rukhsana Ahmed

Nisa looked around nervously as she walked along the dusty edge of the road on that suffocating July afternoon. She was in a part of Lahore which she did not know very well but all the landmarks her neighbour *Apa* Zarina had described had kept appearing so far. She tugged at the *burqa* round her shoulders as if afraid of being recognized through its thin georgette veil and the black silky folds that enveloped her neat, compact little figure. It belonged to her unmarried friend Seema and had been borrowed specially for the occasion. This was the first time in her whole life that she had embarked on a mission knowing it wasn't "permitted". She was trembling slightly with guilt and fear. Her breathing and heartbeat quickened as she approached the house.

Just as Zarina had said, it stood at the end of the *kutchi abadi*. A small house, one of the few here which were brick-built. Right outside its entrance was the lean-to of the motorbike repair shop which she had been told to look out for. Two men sat there tinkering with motorbikes which looked too rusty and battered to be repaired. They looked up from their sweaty labour each time a woman went in or out of the green door of Talat's house.

Most of the women who came had their faces covered with shawls or *dupattas* and some, like Nisa, wore *burqas*. But occasionally the men succeeded in catching a glimpse of a young, fresh, female face. In any case they weren't discouraged by the veils and cloaks. If the outline or gait indicated a youngish woman they did their best to get attention by shouting an obscenity or by humming a snatch of film song.

The women had been trained for years to sidestep and ignore this kind of behaviour. So they all scurried past, hastening their footsteps just a little. Nisa, who was skilled in the same strategy, quickened her pace to reach the shelter of the house although she had been fearful of the ultimate step she was about to take. It was for her a house of Evil.

She stood for a second looking around the bare courtyard. In one corner was the usual outside tap in its sunken cemented square used for washing. All down the courtyard hung the laundry drying at the remarkable speed that only the brilliant afternoon sun made possible. Hesitating for an instant, she walked into the small room beyond.

Her eyes were blinded by the sudden fragrant darkness of the room and she steadied herself against the door jamb as she stumbled over the stock of shoes near the door. Slipping off her own, Nisa sat down just inside the doorway. She gasped as her eyes began to see.

Talat sat on a low stage with two huge black snakes entwined round her body. She was strikingly good-looking and very fashionable. Her large black eyes were highlighted by the blackest of kohl and her small delicate mouth was painted a brilliant red, matching the nail varnish on her carefully manicured hands. A shapely bosom and a slender waist were clearly outlined through her, black lawn *kurta*. She was muttering to herself, eyes closed, body swaying rhythmically, whilst the women round her stared in hypnotized fascination.

Nisa's glance surveyed the room quickly. The sunlight had been shut out. In the dim lamplight she could make out crudely painted pictures of holy faces which she had never seen before. She remembered hearing about distant foreign lands where it was customary to paint portraits of saints, a practice she knew was definitely blasphemous, and she hastily touched her ears in a gesture of contrition. *"Tauba, tauba"*, she sought forgiveness. In one corner burned scented candles emitting whitish clouds of smoke with a cloying sweet smell. On the mantelshelf stood a photo of Talat with her *guru* who looked remarkably young and healthy as he smiled down at her with his hand resting on her head in benediction.

The queue was moving slowly. People were leaving one by one as each managed to get a personal audience with Talat. There was the usual assortment of problems – mother-in-law or daughter-in-law ones, there were patients seeking cures for incurable diseases, the destitute looking for a better future. Whatever their problems, Talat gave them that hope they knew they did not have.

No one seemed to have come alone except Nisa. She trembled again. It would be her turn soon to speak to Talat. She wasn't sure even now what she would say or what she would ask for. She clutched her cheap plastic handbag in a fierce grip under her left arm and in her right hand she held a brown paper bag containing the four eggs she had bought on her way up, according to Zarina's instructions. The sweat from her fingers had formed a damp, dark ring round the base of the paper bag. She wondered uncomfortably if it was going to give way.

As the crowd in the room thinned, Nisa found herself slowly moving nearer to the raised dais. Within half an hour she was face to face with Talat. Nisa looked up into the dark, warm, liquid eyes. Disconcerted by Talat's youthful appearance, she felt for an instant she had made a mistake. Talat's eyes smiled as if they'd read her thoughts.

"How can I help you, my daughter?" she asked, as if a little amused by this belated scepticism. Her manner and her address claimed for herself the supremacy and status which age automatically bestows on everyone in that world, a manner which seemed strangely inappropriate in someone who was perhaps only nineteen or twenty.

But Nisa was overwhelmed by the encouraging sympathy and affection in her voice and felt the tears welling up in her throat. She could only say, "It's my husband . . .", before she broke down into a fit of sobbing, aware that she was being stared at very curiously. This kind of desperation was always useful as it impressed other clients. Talat soothed her gently and tenderly.

"Hush, my daughter, have faith. I can help you." Her voice was reassuring. She eyed the bag in Nisa's hands and asked in a whisper, "Do you want me to do a *chowkie* for you?" Nisa could only nod an affirmative. Talat proceeded quickly to perform that ritual. Relieving Nisa of the eggs she placed them in a neat square on a small wooden stool. Nisa stopped crying as she watched in fascination. Talat's fingers moved dextrously as she placed a bowl beside the stool and then began to unwind the snakes from her body. She pulled both of them up to the eggs and closed her eyes, rocking backwards and forwards as if in a trance.

Nisa's body stiffened with fear as the snakes stood danger-ously close to her for a few seconds, sniffing the eggs and then raising their heads in what looked like vicious contempt. There was absolute silence in the room as everyone watched. Talat came out of her trance and her assistant, a very plain woman of around thirty-five or so, helped her to capture the snakes and put them away in two large, colourful, wicker baskets.

The snakes slithered and hissed as if in protest, but were soon put away. While the other woman was covering the baskets with pieces of black cloth, Talat began to break the eggs one by one into the clay bowl. Nisa tried to watch her but felt compelled to watch the snakes.

Suddenly she heard Talat's voice cursing under her breath and looked fearfully down at the bowl. On top of the cracked eggs floated claws, blood and some strange, noxious and ugly greenish matter.

"Ah, my daughter," Talat exclaimed as she folded her hands and closed her eyes as if to seek help from above. Nisa shuddered and covered her face with both hands in shock and horror.

"You are deep in difficulties, I can see." Talat was shaking her head in concern. "You need the Art to help you. You can change the path of your man, you know. There is a way . . ."

The pitch of her voice had changed. Nisa was shivering visibly now. Talat leaned closer to Nisa. She whispered confidentially in her ears as the other women stared. Nisa had kept the lower half of her veil stretched across her face but the curious audience could see her anxious brown eyes widen with horror as they hung on Talat's face, drinking in her whispered words.

She felt dumbfounded and shaken. With her finger on the clasp of her handbag she looked at Talat's companion and began fumblingly, "What's the . . . the fee? What shall I . . ."

The woman glanced at Talat's face and replied gushingly, "Oh, there's no fee really, *Bibi*. But we do have to take some *nazar*s for the snakes, you know. It's ten rupees for the *chowkie*, *Bibi*." And she continued again quickly, "You know, Talat *Bibi* has to perform a *chilla* many times to get her powers. That's very, very hard work, *Bibi*. And you need *nazar*s for the snakes, you know, *Bibi*. It's twenty-five rupees in all."

She was observing Nisa closely as she spoke, the changing expression in Nisa's eyes guiding her in her reckoning of the bill. Nisa pushed the greasy notes with clumsy and clammy fingers into the assistant's eager hands and stumbled to her feet hastily.

Outside, she tripped over the burning stones in the paved courtyard and then on the threshold of the green door. The two men looked up and jeered again but Nisa neither saw nor heard them. She was too preoccupied with those strange whispered words. She saw the bus approaching from the right direction and ran towards it, relieved at not having to wait in the blistering heat near that evil place.

In all her twenty-six years she had never been so shocked by what she had heard or seen. Neither the shock, years ago, of seeing some pornographic pictures that a girl at school had found in her father's trunk, nor that other time when she had woken up in the middle of the night as the family slept on the roof-top and suddenly realized that the neighbours were actually "doing it" could compare. She had blushed into the pillow and covered her ears to block out the muffled sounds. The mental picture of *Chachi* Nuggo's massive breasts flashed in her mind and the thought of *Chachaji* on top of her embarrassed her even as she remembered it now, almost ten years later.

"It's indecent even to think of it," she reprimanded herself. Her mind returned again to the present and tried to grapple with what Talat had just told her.

"Women," she'd said, "are powerful beings. If you want your man to be utterly in your power all you have to do is give him a drop of your own blood to drink." As Nisa stared at Talat, vaguely apprehensive, she elaborated her meaning. "Menstrual blood has great magical powers, you know. A man can never overcome the spell. He will become a slave to your will."

Nisa shuddered again as she remembered the words with horror and revulsion. The very thought seemed so impure to her, so unclean. She felt certain that the knowledge came from the devil. "I couldn't do such an awful thing, even to Hameed," she mused to herself, wondering longingly for a few seconds about how it would feel if Hameed was indeed a slave to her will. She tried determinedly to shake off the idea.

"*Ammah* was right," she thought. "Never to go to these weird places. They are truly evil . . . there can be no doubt about it."

She really regretted having gone to see Talat. If it hadn't been for Zarina she'd never have done it. "No one really believes in such things these days," she thought. "Yet Zarina's mother does look a lot better now." The justification for the trip also rose from within her heart.

The debate continued in her mind all the way back across town on the bus. It was almost time for *Asar* prayers; the shadows had doubled in length, she noticed, as she got off near the Mini Market and walked round the shops to the row of poky little houses behind them. Her footsteps quickened as she thought of the children being looked after by Zarina.

Her neighbour was full of questions but Nisa could not bring herself to repeat what Talat had told her. She just hedged round the questions and rushed off with her brood, saying she still had the dinner to cook.

She fed the older children and sat down to nurse the younger of her two boys, Zafar. Her mind was still occupied by her afternoon's adventure. She now felt curiously subdued and guilty about it. Zarina had meant well. Indeed, Nisa often felt guilty even about the fact that her neighbours knew the problems she was having with her marriage.

Her mother had always stressed the dignity and value of reserve. "A good woman," she used to say, "knows how to keep the family's secrets. What's the use, anyway, of telling people seven doors away that your month's allowance hasn't quite stretched to the last four days this month? If possible, you manage to survive without letting the world know."

Nisa felt that was indeed where she'd failed to act as a really good wife. Her neighbours on all three sides of her knew her dark secret. Her own family did not know. She was proud of that. Every time someone had come to visit her from her home town, Sialkot, she had kept up appearances quite well. But she hadn't been able to hide the truth from her neighbours.

Each night when Hameed got home, looking drunk and forbidding, she strengthened her resolve to keep out of his way and not to cause a row, but five nights out of ten she failed. He seemed to seek her out as if that was what he'd been waiting for all day. She wished sometimes that he could come home earlier so that the noise of his rowing would be less noticeable. At eleven the whole neighbourhood was quiet and each abusive mouthful he hurled at her could be heard at least three doors away. Sometimes there were flying plates and howling children, if they happened to wake up. A couple of times she had lost control herself and had begun to scream hysterically with fear.

Anyway, she realized that it had got easier for her since the neighbours knew. Sometimes when the row was a really bad one Zarina would call out to ask if she was all right. The shame of that always got through to Hameed, even if he was really drunk, and it made him stop and go to bed grumbling about interfering busybody neighbours.

His anger and abuse were often followed by an overbearingly vicious assertion of his conjugal rights which Nisa never dared to deny him, and she believed she ought not dare to deny him either. She never resisted him but she resented his heavy-handed impatience. She hated the stink of cheap, home-brewed beer on his breath with all the moral weight of her mother's censure of drinking. And she missed the snatches of wooing from the early days of her marriage.

After the day's wearying labour, it was that physical humiliation borne in silence five nights out of ten which was consuming her. She loathed that physical submission to his will. It had to be done like the housework and the caring of the children. It was her part of the deal, her return for the housekeeping allowance. She didn't argue about that but she bitterly resented his drinking. Though she wouldn't dare argue with him, she was unable to conceal her disapproval. And her tight-lipped hostility aggravated his bad temper. He was riled by her strong sense of moral superiority into an even deeper viciousness. Sometimes this worked for her. He would be too angry to want her afterwards. Sometimes he would be too drunk to notice her aloofness or her lofty anger and he just pleased himself.

That evening as she lay on her *charpoy* in the courtyard staring at the clear night sky, a vision of Talat's face kept intruding into her thoughts. It was a picture of Talat which compelled her imagination. She saw her standing waist-deep in the shallower waters of the Ravi, dressed in black, eyes uplifted to the moon, invoking her powers. Power, the very thought of power seemed so seductive to Nisa in her helpless situation. She had been adventurous that morning but she knew she couldn't be as brave as Talat, though she longed to have some control over her circumstances.

She jumped up as she heard Hameed's footsteps at the door. It was nearly eleven, his usual time. She quickly brought the simmering water on the stove to the boil and tipped the rice in. That night as Hameed launched into his usual nagging and complaining between each morsel of curried lentils and rice, Nisa felt her resolve never to think about magic weakening.

She wondered how much pain it took, how much courage, to pollute a man's cup of tea or glass of iced water. She watched Hameed's lips pressed against the glass of water and shivered. Through her mind flashed a memory of her first-born, Karim, newly arrived, lying across her belly, sticky and a little blood-stained. She had touched him unbelievingly . . . the sight of the drops of blood on the cord hadn't really worried her or repulsed her then. That was the clot of blood that had made him possible, given him life.

"What are you staring at?" Hameed snapped peevishly, and Nisa jumped to her feet again to clear up the plates. Somewhere in the recesses of her mind she had caught a glimpse of herself performing a grossly sacrilegious spell and that glimpse had unnerved her for a few seconds.

All her life she had seen the women around her observing the taboos in this area of their lives. Nisa herself had developed a deep sense of shame over the years through the secrecy and the avoidances. Now it was as though Talat had pulled out a vital brick at the base of that belief.

If it really had magical powers, why did women abhor it so, she wondered. She knew she was too simple to work out the

answers but the question rose insistently within her heart each
month when she menstruated. The abhorrence didn't make sense
to her now that she thought about it. After all, they all knew
enough about the physical aspect of menstruation. Wasn't there
some mild relief when girls "started" or worry when they were
"late"?

Seven months passed by with the creeping pace of a prison
sentence. Each month she wondered if she would dare. Each
month when the moon was full she remembered Talat's eyes, her
face aglow in the moonlight standing waist-deep in the waters of
the Ravi, and each month the spell seemed less shocking, She
thought about herself, her life and her body a great deal in those
months. Each time she saw the moon she prayed for a better
month, but things did not change. Except for her own attitude to
her own body. That changed subtly.

Towards the end of the month, when the money began to
run out on the twenty-fifth or thereabouts, a deep bitterness filled
her heart. She had to turn to him again to ask him for more and
have him spit in her face. They'd always been the worst nights of
the month, when his anger had a sharper, more righteous edge to
it. But now when that happened she resented him as deeply as he
resented the increased expenses.

She had grown weary of her life. The skimping and the
managing, the hard work and the violence and finally the humiliating abuse of her body. She began to refuse him. That was the way
of wayward women, she'd been taught, but she no longer cared.

Hameed was nonplussed by her refusal, too surprised and
hurt to argue or insist at first. But then she began to reject him
more frequently and he had to react. Surprisingly, he did not take
her forcibly, but became more violent in other ways. It was
almost as if he was aware of her newly found veneration for her
own body, and had to violate her in some other way.

For Nisa those refusals became a small triumph each time.
The black eyes, the swollen lips or bruised face became more

commonplace for her. Zarina's mother would shake her head sadly sometimes and say, "Oh, that man, *Beti*. God will reward you for your patience. What makes him so angry?"

For Nisa the bruises became an option she preferred to humiliating sex. She wasn't sure that she wanted rewards in heaven; she only wished she had to suffer less on earth.

That spring Zarina's mother became ill again. The doctor came but the old lady was not reassured. She kept talking of Talat and how well her remedy had worked the year before. Nisa came back from their house with her head full of memories of the day she had gone to see Talat.

Talat was no longer an evil practitioner of magic for her. She appeared in her memory as someone gentle and loving, a friend and a sympathizer, who cared for the underdog, for her. The knowledge that Talat had imparted to her of the strange, sinful spell had given her a sense of strength. Nisa had changed from being a shivering, huddled creature into a calmer, thinking woman.

That evening was women's night out. Seema was getting married the next day. They were all getting together to assemble her clothes for her trousseau, ready to be shown to the in-laws the following day. Nisa had found the right moment to obtain Hameed's permission to attend. She went round early, dressed in glittering clothes, her best earrings swinging from her ears, Zafar in her arms and the older two trailing by her side.

The girls were in high spirits, the singing was buoyant and loud. Nisa tried hard to blend into the scene but her laughter was laboured. The same old familiar well-loved tunes were jarringly painful today. The lies they told of marital bliss, of loving husbands and contented days irritated her. Nisa looked around at the little house sadly and remembered her mother's house. She was pulled out of her nostalgia by the sound of Seema's aunt lecturing her on how to cope with her new life. Forbearance and forgiveness were the operative words. That too was all too familiar.

Nisa could restrain herself no longer. She suddenly erupted, "And how much exactly is she really supposed to endure, *Chachi*? How many tears does it take to make a home?" She asked quietly, "If Seema was really drowning in her own tears and being choked by her own screams, would you still not want her to look back to this house?"

Looking a little uncomfortable and annoyed, the aunt said, "Heaven forbid, rather an inauspicious question for tonight, isn't it?"

Other women around them showed an interest in the conversation. Most of them knew about Nisa. Suddenly Nisa felt an arm around her shoulders. It was Seema's mother. The pain beneath the question had communicated itself to her. "No mother could shut her doors behind her daughter forever. If Seema needed help, I would gladly let her in, of course."

Nisa smiled with difficulty and returned to the kitchen for another teapot. Zarina was assisting in the kitchen.

"You know what?" she chirped as she saw Nisa coming in. "I went to Talat's house today to get Anunah's medicine and I found to my great surprise that Talat and her family have disappeared."

"What do you mean?"

"Well, packed up and shot off into the night."

"Why?" Nisa's heart was throbbing.

"Well! The motorcycle mechanic said they had to run because too many people kept returning to demand their money back. It seems she was a fraud."

Nisa was quiet as she walked the short distance back home with Zarina. The children were exhausted. She took their shoes off one by one and then went into the kitchen to cook the rice, still wondering about Talat. At times she could have sworn that she actually felt the power of the magic, the spell she carried within her body. Now she felt lost and bereft again. She kept hoping that the spell she knew about was genuine.

Hameed came in later and more drunk than ever. He attacked her more viciously than usual, taunting her about her finery and the earrings. Nisa, overwrought and frightened, got up hurriedly to leave the room but he pulled her by the arm. She lost her balance, stumbled and fell to the floor. Her head hit the corner of the wooden *chowkie* and began to bleed furiously. There was a terrible clang as enamelled mugs, plates and bowls rolled off the kitchen shelf. The noise shook Hameed. He pulled himself up and tried to help Nisa up.

But she was hysterical. "No! No! No!" she was screaming. "Don't touch me! Don't come near me. I'll kill you. I'll stab you. I'll poison you." Words poured out of her as fast as the blood sprang from her wound. She looked strange in her glittering clothes, blood-stained face and dishevelled hair.

Zarina was knocking on the door furiously. Hameed, bemused and shaken, let her in and went out again himself. At once Zarina took charge. She nursed Nisa's injuries, calmed her down and helped her to bed. The children had slept through the commotion.

The next morning when Nisa woke up everything was quite clear in her head. She knew what she had to do. She packed some things for herself and Zafar in a small steel trunk. The older children were at school. They walked there and back with Zarina's children. She stood on a small stool near the wall and called Zarina to tell her.

"I'm going to my mother's house, *Apa*," she said. "I'm taking Zafar with me. I don't think they will turn us away. If nothing else, I can wash dishes and cook. If Hameed cannot keep Safia and Karim let him drop them off in Sialkot as well."

Zarina nodded tearfully and promised to keep an eye on them for her. For once she did not have the courage to persuade Nisa that she must endure and that he would change. She didn't know of a magic which worked. Nisa had seen a vision she could not forget, she'd felt a power she could not deny. As she turned away and walked out of the courtyard, clutching both Zafar and the silver trunk, her steps were laboriously slow but firm and determined.

Originally written in English

The Testimony
Afzal Tauseef

The case had been held up for four years. And all the while the accused were kept in dingy cells in the Old Fort. They had been declared dangerous terrorists even before their trial. Thousands had already been punished. Summary military courts had announced sentences within two or three days. Hanging, flogging, harsh imprisonment, confiscation of property. The major-judge would decide whatever he thought fair.

In that respect, this was a peculiar case. Four years spent in jail undergoing torture and hardship. Intelligent, courageous, clever, their crime was unwavering nationalism – this was the reason for their imprisonment.

None of them was a Buddha or had a desire to become the next Christ. But they had left the comforts of their homes because they had wanted to share the anguish of the masses. Plucking out thorns was no easy task but they had to rise in resistance because injustice had increased in the world. Those living on the banks of rivers would keep dying of thirst so long as the ones with guns and power controlled how water was used.

The men had wanted to alleviate the tribulations of Mother Earth. And Mother Earth – looted and plundered for generations – looked to her sons for vindication. There was nobody left to safeguard her honour. Indeed, most of the scions had abandoned her. The elite went off and joined forces with the enemy. Pimps traded the honour of their land to flaunt gold and silk. Some turned into rogues, others smugglers. The masters used them well.

The most evil-looking were given guard duties, and the rest were turned into lackeys. The masters kept control by attaching gold chains to the silver collars hung round lackeys' necks. Control over the entire land lay in their hands. Guns ruled the fields and streets. Motor-cars choked the face of the Earth Mother.

No one was permitted to breathe. It had always been a police state but this time the system was pitiless. No one was allowed to have principles or follow his own culture.

A new Gestapo had taken the place of the dead and departed colonial system, and the nation was once again a neo-colonial state.

Despite it all, mothers did not stop giving birth to sons. Faith in God remained. One could still find human beings. There was still hope, and stars still shone. People yearn for light. They heard that there was a new sun in the world and a new thought. They heard of new dreams. The message of hope wafted in, undetected, with the early morning breeze. The Gestapo could imprison men and make them disappear forever, it could burn books of inspiration and it could incarcerate writers; but how could it hold captive the fragrance of hope?

The chief of the Gestapo promulgated an ordinance: "Hope is a dangerous thing. It must not be allowed to spread!" How? The Gestapo intellectuals suggested that despair be spread amongst the masses. And various agencies began this unholy task. The suffocation increased to such a level that it became hard to breathe. All potential sources of hope were destroyed. But hope had become one with the wind, it could not be killed. Trailing the path of hope, the Gestapo would report on its destination. Arrests began, warrants were issued, death now stretched to infinity. And the light in the eyes of mothers became dull.

But neither despair nor the fear of death would affect those who had once smelled the fragrance of hope. Many such dauntless men filled the cells of the prison. Such were the twenty-one young men who had been awaiting trial for four years. They were familiar with all degrees of torture meted out in the Old Fort, but they had stayed alive and they had not let go of hope. These valiant men, stars taunting the black devil night, were themselves a ray of hope.

They were arrested at midnight. It was an ordinary, routine arrest. But what was singular in their case was that they were being kept for four years without a trial. A lot had transpired in those four years. Countless trials and thousands of decisions. Imprisonment, torture, executions – all in seconds: for the military courts had a lot to accomplish. There was a massive battle going on between the armed Oppressor and the unarmed Oppressed. Armed with only truth, the oppressed would die fighting. The prisoners of this war kept on increasing until one day the jails had no more room. And so black holes were created.

A lot of military courts had come into operation and there were countless gallows but it seemed that these twenty-one young men still had some time to go. Finally, after full fifty months, their trial began. The world press reported: "Freedom Fighters Face Trial!" At least it was better than the fate of countless others who were arrested at night, executed in the morning and buried without ceremony. Not even a poet got to hear what fate they had met. "We who died amongst unlit paths."

They too were to die but not without an uproar. A long charge-sheet had been drawn up with all the charges originating from a single accusation: that these men, who had grown up amid despair, wished to triumph over the forces of darkness. Although they had been given fifty months to think it over not one of them compromised. For them life meant a life of hope and light, a life that would vanquish the darkness which had descended over the land.

It used once to be said that nothing could deflect the rays of the sun. That is true no more. The latest technology has been developed to perpetrate inhumanity and injustice and that technology is operated here. Such extravagant lies of this New Age: for the last decade this land has come under the sway of the King of Lies. Black clouds hover between sun and land. The masters of lies, Satans of this earth, prevent the blessings of nature from reaching the masses. Blessings? New sunshine and fresh rain. People yearn for them in this dismal land. Below the surface the water has turned bitter and above it the atmosphere is full of despair.

It was difficult to survive. One entire decade. Some became ill, others suffocated. Many became blind and dumb. Those young men accused and awaiting trial, they too grew up in this era of the technology of falsehood and oppression. This technical sophistication had taken over the Third World like an epidemic of smallpox. But the young men could still see and talk and hear. In fact, they knew all about hope.

The Gestapo had grown suspicious because the technology to cut through darkness had been brought to the country and men already skilled in its use were prepared to act. If the sun comes out and the rain falls, then the dumb start speaking and the blind are able to see. If Moses grows up in Pharaoh's home, it means the death of the Pharaoh. That is why the new Pharaohs stay alert. The dogs of the Gestapo barked danger. Alarms were sounded. There was danger to the life of the King of Darkness. Danger to his Kingdom, to his supremacy. But how did this come about? How could their system fail, the masters and servants asked each other. Asked themselves. For in their estimation the land had turned barren. All the sons of the mother killed. This time even Assiya Rani was behind bars. The borders had been sealed. Only smuggled goods and heroin crossed borders – those too in army vehicles.

The masters were upset by only one thing. No system had yet been devised to seal the borders of thought. What happened next? Full four years were spent in the investigations. The beliefs of the accused had developed in this very land – developed by some Assiya Mai – but they must somehow have got hold of the technology that cut through the darkness from some enlightened country. Which one? Take any name from the list of enemy countries. Yes, that's right. That's the best way to develop a sensational conspiracy, to make strong accusations. Everyone is happy. Masters and the masters of the masters. What more do they want? That is why they had to set up a special stage for the trial. Had it been a simple internal matter, the judge of the summary court would have thrown them into the slaughter machine with the rest. There would have been no need for witnesses or evidence. But then they themselves miscalculated by making the involvement of the other country known to the public. They got caught in their own trap.

In fact they had wished to prove that the land could not give birth to strong people. Those born here are blind and in this land of darkness, the seeing eye – vision – must come from outside. Terrorism Article so-and-so, Conspiracy Article so-and-so, Treason Article so-and-so, all these words of abuse were brought together to form a charge-sheet. The emperor without clothes had gone out with his procession. But here, instead of a procession, they used newspapers. Yet the press of the free world itself recognized the fraud behind their offering. So they had to bring in witnesses and evidence.

Is it a conspiracy to fight for your independence? The Gestapo says it is a crime. But the world does not agree. There should be some measure of truth. If not a foreign hand, then at least its presses should be there. The agencies of the Gestapo were powerful, certainly, but it is not easy to hoodwink the entire international press. They had to make the case look real. The witnesses may not be genuine but they should at least look genuine. The Gestapo had to execute these freedom fighters to safeguard its own prestige. Not one out of the twenty-one had agreed to turn state witness, not even when the stakes were life and death. First, they were genuine people; second, who would have wanted to let a Satanic organization like the Gestapo have access to their souls? Who wants to die for Satan?

Treason and sacrifice are far apart and between the two lie oceans of regret. Many more months went by. The Gestapo was unable to find witnesses.

So what happened next? They found witnesses. After fifty months they got hold of eye-witnesses of the conspiracy. The witnesses seemed real enough and all the rest was accomplished by the Gestapo.

Years before, their passports, stamped with a visa for that particular country, had been stolen. A man and a woman. Both of them had visited that country on business. But the Gestapo didn't worry about such details. It just needed evidence.

The witnesses were also arrested at midnight like the accused. After the "civilized" arrest they were introduced to the pleasures of the torture chambers, death row, solitary confinement. While they experienced these atrocities, their families were also crushed.

Once ready, they were released. The condition being: "If you refuse to give the correct testimony, you will be brought back." Can anyone believe this today? That such atrocities took place in the eighty-fourth year of the twentieth century. But why not? In this small country of the Third World it is just another small blackmail. It was all very clever actually. Both were from the lower middle class, educated and with families. They belonged to a class which would rather stay subservient than jeopardize its honour. Fear and trepidation were their life-style. Typical examples of the white-collared class. The woman witness was in the worse position. The sole earning member of the family, she was educating her children and trying to keep up a front of respectability. The honour that she had earned, however, was so important to her, she could easily have given her life for it.

The two witnesses were made to sign a bond to give testimony when asked and to ensure complete secrecy. The least indiscretion was threatened with dangerous consequences. People from the intelligence shadowed them throughout the long wait. They kept quiet for many months but for how long could they question their inner voice? There was a conflict within. Between falsehood and truth. Shall we compromise or remain steadfast and die? There could be only two outcomes to the conflict. Either sell their souls to the enemy or fight to the death. What a choice!

The conflict within the woman was more vicious. There was a crisis raging inside. This testimony is a testimony of falsehood and treason. It is going to send brave men to the gallows and compromise all your principles. A voice screamed within her: "Listen. Do not consent to be enslaved by Satan. Do not betray mankind. These brave men are like my sons. My son may not be a hero but he is the light of my eyes, the comfort of my heart, just as these prisoners are the hope of this land. Where shall I shelter if I testify against them? How shall I live afterwards? This land will never forgive me, but if I refuse, if I deny: what then? What then? Who will save me? Shall I have to leave this country? Many people have gone into exile – refugees.

"No, this way out is very difficult, I cannot leave my own land. What then is the easy way out? I could never pay back what I owe to this land. My ancestors never compromised. There is too much at stake for me to stand up to these evil forces. My son's life, my daughter's honour, my livelihood and my shelter. Dear God, I have nowhere to go. You have made them so powerful. Tell me, how am I to withstand them? This is not the first time it has happened. Only this time, it is my turn."

She would think over all these things. All the things one could die or live for. "There are so many obligations, so many responsibilities. Had I been single I could have survived but in what way are my son and daughter to blame? Why should their lives be ruined? Oh, my Creator, if ever I should meet you I would ask if such dangers had ever existed before."

Sometimes she would be decided not to give testimony. "My son is just my son but there are very few lion-hearted men left. They are the honour of this land. Their lives are very precious. But are they more precious than the honour of my daughter?" This question would break her resolve.

"It is unjust. I have not been dealt a fair hand. I cannot sacrifice my honour, but what should I do? I stand between the devil and the deep blue sea. Oh please, grant me some respite."

But there was no respite. Six months passed in this conflict. The time had almost come. The time for testimony. Would it be preceded by an earthquake, a flood or a storm?

"Before my soul is sold to Satan why does my heart not stop beating? By making us human beings you have constrained us. You have allowed everyone to be called human. Even those who find entertainment in the distress of their fellow beings. Are you really All Powerful? Do not wrench me apart from my land. Do not let the land and myself feel shame for each other. We have always played the role of protectors. Do not spoil it, please. Do not let me be a traitor."

She talked to herself endlessly in this way. But now time was passing quickly. Sometimes she would imagine herself as a Gestapo witness testifying against the freedom fighters. It would make her entire being tremble. Her inner turmoil was now reflected in her physical self. No one knew what was troubling her. At times she would recall her mother saying: "Little one, you were born at the blessed hour of dawn. There is nothing that you cannot have if you pray for it." Then what had gone wrong now?

A weak, lonely woman given such a big responsibility. She herself did not know that she was fighting the battle between good and evil. No one knew why she could not sleep at night nor why she wept at dawn. No one could be told that she had to give evidence. Days, nights, seconds. The six months had turned into six centuries. It seemed to her as if she had been carrying that burden of anguish for hundreds of years. Her physical being shrank with grief. She yearned for death. It made her happy. Please God help take my life away. Dust unto dust. Soul to soul. Let my soul shine on some far-off star. The Gestapo would never be able to reach out there. This idea resolved her inner crises.

She even asked a learned man if one could achieve death through will-power. The learned one replied, "Will-power can never be a negative force. But through it you can conquer death." That night she dreamt that she spoke with those brave prisoners. Like proud lions they sat behind bars. Two days before, their photographs had been published in a foreign magazine. "Young lions awaiting death." The caption said a lot but they sat in silence. She heard them in her dream. "Mother, do not worry about us. Give them the testimony which they want without fear. We are vindicated alive or dead. We have not compromised and have chosen this life ourselves and have chosen death ourselves. We want something else from you. Come to the court for the testimony but record this story for time. For tomorrow. So that tomorrow our young brothers and sisters do not remain ignorant of the truth. So that they do not think our generation did not struggle, did not make sacrifices. So that nobody can say this generation produced only pimps and slaves. Even after taking your testimony, they can kill you, so take care of yourself. Mother, take care of yourself for the sake of tomorrow. You must be a witness to our struggle. It would be great if a respectable woman like yourself would bear testimony to our struggle."

"Sons, blessings. May your mothers be proud of you. How easy you have made my life."

All this conflict took place only on one side; the other witness had decided to give his testimony quite early on. He had decided to save his family. He could do nothing for anyone else. This was the routine consideration of that time. It was an insensitive, suffocating time and all the sensitive souls were behind bars. The history of slavery is made up of many similar occasions. There was a time when only Abraham stood with God.

So for the male witness it was an easy job. He had to say yes to the masters. Give his testimony. A completely false, lying testimony to save himself and his family. He might live a few more days, this way. His family would flourish while the visionaries would be executed. It would have happened in any case. So many had been executed in the last decade. So many imprisoned for life. A flood of terror was overtaking all of mankind. The flood had uprooted even big strong trees and only the few who could resist the flood were left.

The day of the testimony arrived. Statements of both witnesses were formulated by the Gestapo. The two had simply to take the oath and read the statement. Where and when? It was kept secret. It came at midnight; a black car came to pick up the witnesses. And they travelled many hundreds of miles. Dead quiet. The car travelled through the night. The woman kept quiet. The guards were also quiet. No one was allowed to talk. Even if it had been permitted, who would they have talked to? Every one was afraid, of each other. The journey came to an end in the morning and the car stopped when it reached the seat of power.

The seat of power was also under the same sky. Birds flew around freely. The witnesses were taken to a room inside the Gestapo headquarters. They were ordered to have breakfast and freshen up, so that they might look normal in the court. The man did so and ate a big breakfast of eggs and bread. The woman drank a cup of tea mingled with her tears. Then they were taken in down a long corridor. Perhaps the trial was taking place within the jail. They passed a great many iron gates. In one barracks sat six or seven men behind desks, with greed dancing in their eyes. These hyena-faced men were members of the Gestapo high command. They opened their files and the lesson began. They were shown the photographs of the brave ones, fourteen and seven. Both cases were the same, the only difference was of time.

The testimony took place separately. Conspiracy, the plan to murder the masters . . . to sabotage their power . . . to overthrow the government. They were told they had to identify the men and they had better not make mistakes. Their statement was going to be of conspiracy, murder and planned insurrection. The woman felt as if she was surrounded by wolves, all the knowledge gleaned from centuries of civilization had got lost somewhere. She felt as if all these cannibals were after her blood. All her children were in great danger. Her children whose photographs were before her. Her children. She had to bear testimony about the first fourteen. All these bright faces. Lively eyes. Tariq, Asher, Aarnir, Sabir, Kamran, Shahzad, Nabil, Nadeem. These were the names of human beings. These were the photographs of human beings. She remembered when her own son was in the cradle. She had named him herself seven days after his birth. It was a name that meant happiness, hope, light and peace. She had wanted to call her son by all these names. But today she realized that she had many more sons. There was a mother inside her. Through the photographs she was still tied to civilization. The world had not disappeared in a whirlpool.

"What are you thinking, woman," a hyena barked. "Keep to your testimony or else your own son will be brought in here." Other hyenas also started looking at her in anger. But to her they seemed like savages sitting there; bloodthirsty savages. She turned numb for a while and then her insides started trembling. But her soul was making its own judgements about mankind. "How innocent these sons of man look even in photographs."

The hyenas conferred with each other and one of them took her aside to test her. "Take an oath on God. Place your hands on the Holy Book. Give the name of your father and family and say, 'I will tell the truth and nothing but the truth'." Conspiracy . . . revolt . . . murder . . . treason . . . terrorism . . . Gathering courage, she fixed her eyes on the hyena and said, "Permit me to ask why I should take an oath on the Holy Book for an unholy testimony?"

"Stop this nonsense and don't try to be clever. Do what you're told. Can't you take the name of God in this testimony?" His mouth was spouting foul spittle. "All right, we will bring your daughter over here, she will be able to give better testimony." The woman felt as though she stood on burning embers. Just at that moment a terrible gong sounded. Tun-dan-dan tun. Was this the trumpet of Judgement Day?

She was sitting in the court. Thank God, it is better to walk than stand on embers. She walked but the burning coal under her feet started insisting. Uphold the truth. Remember all those who made friends with the fire of truth? All those who went to the gallows for it? One of them stood and carried his own cross. The others? The Resurrected Messiah. With a poison chalice to his lips, Socrates. A little ahead with his bloodstained clothes was another defender of truth, alone in Karbala, Hussain Ibn Ali.

She was walking along deep in thought, when the Gestapo guard poked her. Turn right, woman. The court is on this side. Then he laughed and said, "You were going towards the execution hole." "Execution hole?" "Yes, this path leads straight to the gallows."

"Why does the straight path lead to the gallows? Why not toward life? Have paths forgotten their destinations?" she again started thinking.

Through the open door she saw the courts. A uniformed officer, flanked by more uniforms, was the judge. "They look less dangerous than the Gestapo." She felt a little relieved. But there was the advocate for the Gestapo. The devil. He was the one who had taken her statement. "Help me, God," she prayed for strength and entered the room. Chan, chan, chan. A great many iron chains clanged together. The accused were being brought in. A great many eyes locked on to her face at the same time. "Wonder what they are thinking of." She also looked at all the faces. Such beauty. Such bright faces. The court officials, hard-featured and vile. It was a strange clash. The young men were standing with full courage and valour; the stars in a dark house.

"It is not I but you who are being tested, God. Give me strength. Keep me on the path of truth."

The statement began. She took the oath. Gave the names of her father and family and placed her hands on the Holy Book. Her statement was being recorded. "They were not part of any conspiracy. In fact, it was a conspiracy that was committed against them."

She kept speaking. An hour, two hours, four hours. She did not stop. The day ended, time bowed. By the time the testimony was finished she was born anew. Her soul had survived fear and now shone against a bright and shining backdrop. The sun bowed before her.

With chains in their hands, standing in a row, the brave ones watched her leave. One of them stepped forward. He had a red rose in one hand and in the other a scrap of paper. There was a message on the paper written in blood. It said: "Mother, all praise to you. Praise to your truth. A rose of the jail to salute your determination." The woman touched her eyes with the rose and left. The hyena was watching her. "Now wait for the consequences. You cannot run, after flouting our orders," he screeched. But threats had no meaning now. She looked at the hyena with fearless eyes and then she remembered the other witness. He had come from another room after giving his testimony. Pale and trembling. Death played on his face and he was unable to look up. His testimony would send seven freedom fighters to the gallows. As a reward he would receive a plot of land. But he was the one who had died.

Originally translated from the Urdu
by Ayesha Haroon

Many Faces of Truth

Bano Qudsia

It was as if a whale had suddenly reared up, such was the impact the vast church had on Ghulam Mohammad when he first caught sight of it on the way from Thamesworth. By that time the car had turned towards the market, so he did not see the "For Sale" sign on its great door. The next time Ghulam Mohammad and his teenage daughter were walking past, on their way to buy groceries, his steps halted of their own accord in front of the church.

"You go on ahead, Poppy. I'll follow you in a minute!" Poppy, a strapping young lady, clad in jeans, walked on, whistling like a boy.

Previously, Ghulam Mohammad had lived in the Marble Arch area of London. He had never chanced to come to this neighbourhood of Birmingham before. But recently he had launched a hotel up there in partnership with one of his kinsmen. These two had once gone back to Pakistan together, making the journey to their village from the Bani Bangla railway station in a horse-drawn carriage.

He was well acquainted with Central London but was totally new to Birmingham. He might well have walked on past after glancing at the church, but the "For Sale" placard on the ebony door of the church held his feet to the ground. The followers of the idea of Trinity had given the building a triangular shape.

Both slopes of the roof were three-cornered. The church had an ebony framework and walls of greyish-black stone. The bay windows had delicate arches adorned with stained glass. The stone footpaths around the church were overgrown with wild grasses, ferns, maidenhair and many other kinds of bushes and shrubs. Ghulam Mohammad took out his handkerchief and as he tried to clean one of the window panes, it shattered to pieces and fell inside. Scared, Ghulam looked around to see if there was anyone who might have caught him damaging public property, but nobody could be seen.

Ghulam Mohammad peeped inside the building. The images of Mary and Christ painted on glass were right in front of him. Otherwise, the place had a desolate, stale, grief-ridden silence. Although there was no dust on the pews and the organ was also clean, it seemed as if no one had come to pray in that church for a long time. The carpeting in the aisle was so worn out it had lost its colour completely and was all creased up.

Avoiding the overgrowth, Ghulam Mohammad walked along beside the wall of the building and found another "For Sale" sign on the side facing the road. For a long time he stood staring at the sign.

Ghulam Mohammad was like a flintstone. With a little friction he produced sparks. Extraordinary ideas, incredible dreams, changing seasons, fantastic architecture, chance meetings with strangers, unexplored places, modern inventions, all kindled his imagination and gave him food for thought. Even when he had lived in his small village, Subhagay, seven miles from Bani Bangla, he had been the same. His companions thought that by going to London he was fleeing from poverty, but Ghulam Mohammad himself was convinced that he had settled at Marble Arch in pursuit of a dream.

All through the day, he sat in his hotel office lost in thought. In the evening too, instead of doing the accounts himself, he placed the cash, the accounts register and the calculator in front of Sikandar, who raised his eyebrows in puzzlement. Ghulam Mohammad was uncompromisingly honest where money dealings were concerned but was generous enough not to count the pennies when offering charity.

"What's the matter?" Sikandar asked. "Aren't you going to check the accounts today?"

"No." said Ghulam Mohammad after a while, staring absent-mindedly at the red chairs of the Birmingham Pakistan Hotel.

"Aren't you feeling well?" his kinsman asked.

"No, it's not that."

"Then what's bothering you?"

"I want to sell my share in this hotel."

Sikander felt a shiver run through him as if a black cat had crossed his path.

"Do you wish to invest in some better venture?"

"No."

"Then may I ask why you need the money?"

"I want to buy a church!"

"A church?" Sikandar wondered if living in exile for fifteen years had caused Ghulam Mohammad to lose his senses.

"I'll convert the church into a mosque. Children will recite the *Koran* there. Ladies will say their prayers in the upper portion and *Maulvi Sahib* will deliver the sermon on Fridays." Sikandar was convinced that it hadn't been such a good idea after all to dislodge Ghulam Mohammad from Marble Arch. He thought his kinsman had gone crazy and was finding it impossible to settle in Birmingham.

"Why are you staring at me like that? Wasn't the Cordoba Mosque converted into a church? I've seen it myself – with these two eyes!" Ghulama growled.

"They could do it there, as the whole population had turned Christian! They didn't need a mosque any more – the white race can do it – they have the money!"

"I now belong to the moneyed class too. I can also do it. If money is the criterion, then I have enough money of my own to do it."

"Let's go to Hirnam Singh's house and stop playing the fool!"

Hirnam Singh was an old friend of Sikandar's. It was Sikandar's custom to greet his friend loudly in the typical Sikh fashion, and his friend, his wife, Jurnail Kore, and his two daughters would greet him back affectionately in the same way.

Sikandar dragged Ghulam Mohammad with him. Reflecting his rural background, Hirnam Singh's house was a jumble of modern conveniences mixed with old traditions and customs. Proudly Jurnail Kore served them corn-bread and spinach. She kept on insisting that the buttermilk was not as good as that made by her mother but at least the spinach tasted almost the same.

Seated in that Birmingham apartment, Sikandar and Hirnam Singh talked for hours about crops, oxen and milk-producing buffaloes. They recalled the village peasants, the artisans, the entertainers, the boys roaming in fields, the carts, the old women tending their mud ovens, children hanging by their arms and women pulling them along, tiny lamps which used mustard oil as fuel and old men clearing their throats. Their umbilical cord was not yet severed from their native fields. Hirnam Singh's daughters sat with them for a little while and then excused themselves. Jurnail Kore kept on laughing noisily, showing her broad teeth. In spite of having lived in Birmingham for so many years, she had not yet learnt to speak softly or laugh in a ladylike manner. Ghulam took absolutely no interest in the conversation of the two friends. Hunched up, he sat watching the 45-inch TV on which some movie was being screened. His eyes were focused on the screen yet all he could see was the floor of the church carpeted in red, with copies of the *Koran* open on their wooden stands, young children making the guttural sounds of Arabic with aplomb, and the air scented with burning incense. After a long while, when they were leaving, Jurnail Kore spoke to Sikandar in thick Punjabi, "Does your friend always keep so quiet or has he got troubles?" Embellishing the story freely with foul language, Sikandar told his friends of Ghulam's trouble in a humorous tone. Jurnail Kore laughed heartily displaying all her teeth. Hirnam Singh said, "Man, my friend, has progressed far ahead of the church, the mosque and the temple. Wipe these obsolete philosophies from your mind. If you visit our country, you will see the mosques in ruins everywhere. Some are being used as stables, others have been turned into offices. Not a single mosque in the villages is properly used. When your people lived there, we could hear the call of the *muezzin* regularly. My father Gordyal Singh used to go out for his walk when he heard the call for morning prayers. Now the only sound emanating from the mosque is the braying of donkeys."

This brought forth a spurt of laughter from Jurnail Kore but Ghulam Mohammad was shaken to the core. A stout man with layers of fat, he felt as if somebody had splashed a bucket of cold water over him.

Lying in bed later on he felt as if he was burning with fever. He kept covering himself with a blanket, and then gulping down water; he would shiver and shake and then place his pillow over his trembling head. Hajra, his wife, had never seen him in such a state. In the dim glow of the street light, she waited for his restlessness to abate but finally she could not help asking him what was wrong. The answer she received made her think that the old man was suffering from acute stress. She massaged his head with oil but still he could not fall asleep. He kept harping on the same theme that he wanted to sell up everything and convert the church into a mosque.

"Have we come to England for the sole purpose of renovating a church? If you desire it so much, then go and live in the village mosque! Hand your business over to your sons and move back to the village. You're needlessly driving me mad too at this unearthly hour!"

Ghulam Mohammad sat up in bed and said with passion, "My good woman! No matter what kind of house is inhabited with God's name, it is good. Don't you see that God is giving us an opportunity! It has been ordained thus! By the grace of God, our sons are now well able to take care of themselves. You must let me do what I want." This plea hit Hajra's brain like a bullet.

"Is it our business to look after God's house? Can you reinhabit the churches of Russia? Go and see the state they have fallen into there! Mrs Waheed was telling me yesterday – she has been there and has seen them all! Are you going to be able to preserve every single church? Look at the temples, the mosques! In how many countries are the Houses of God in disrepair? It's not one country or one building. Is it only one nation that has forgotten God? Look after your own house. Your own children may not forgive you. Think of your youngest son and let God take care of his own House!"

Ghulam Mohammad closed his eyes. He was the captive of a dream. He couldn't heed Hajra's injunctions. He felt he would die if he couldn't buy the church. The last time, when he was leaving his village, Subhagay, his kinsfolk had tried hard to persuade him not to do it and at that time too he had felt that he would die if he did not leave for England. Before embarking on his journey, he had gone to the mosque to bid farewell to *Maulvi Sahib*. He was resting on a straw mat after leading the afternoon prayers. There was a dearth even of straw mats in the tumbledown village mosque and people were used to saying their prayers on the mud floor, just spreading out a handkerchief over the spot where their head touched the ground.

"What brings you here, Ghulam Mohammad?"

"*Maulvi Sahib*, I'm leaving Karachi soon," he said, feeling the presence of the green passport in his pocket.

"Your heart then is adamant!"

"It seems so."

"What will you do for a living over there?"

"Labouring work for some time, and then whatever God wishes me to do."

"If you accept God as a bestower even here, then . . ." *Maulvi Sahib* smiled behind his beard.

Ghulam Mohammad remained silent. He had meant to say farewell to *Maulvi Sahib* and had no intention of changing his decision. For a long time he sat there chewing on a straw.

"Subhagay's population has halved since everyone started leaving for England. Whom will I call for prayers if everybody forsakes the village? Who will come to the mosque if there is no one around?"

Ghulama realized that he could never go back to the village to breathe new life into the House of God there. His roots might not be so firmly fixed in England but his four children were incapable of making Subhagay their home. The elder two remained in London while he had asked Nazeer and Poppy to come with him. His children were no longer at the stage where they would listen to their elders, nor were they aware of a culture in which the elders had to be obeyed. They were not even like the local people, who followed a given way of life. They had turned out a peculiar mixture of too much England and too little Subhagay.

While chewing gum, Poppy and Nazeer listened to their father. After a long introduction and a lot of scolding from Hajra who wanted him to come to the point, Ghulam Mohammad said, "I've sold my hotel share. My four shops in London, I bequeath to you four children. Whatever I have retained, I plan to use it to give new life to the old church."

Removing an imaginary speck of dust from her jeans, Poppy said, "But *Abbaji*, it's a church and has been a church for two hundred years! We don't have any right to do anything to it. Let the Christians decide what they want to do with it."

The argument was logical. It clashed with Ghulam Mohammad's dream and another piece of glass shattered. But

Ghulam Mohammad was single-minded in the pursuit of his dream. He was not confounded by this superficial piece of logic for long.

"Poppy dear, wherever the House of God is, it should be inhabited – every mosque, every temple. We won't get anywhere if we forget this. We should keep on coming to the House of God, even if not regularly, at least now and then. If . . . if I am able to create a mosque here, just think of the number of children who would be able to recite the *Koran* and if we are determined, maybe – just maybe – we'll one day hear the call for prayers as well. Then other nationalities might join us and who knows whether perhaps bit by bit every . . ."

He became so emotional that he could not go on, but he also stopped because he could not face the icy looks of his children, and lapsed into silence.

It is said that on the day of the National Front march when thugs fired bullets in a Birmingham market area and set fire to four houses, Ghulam Mohammad's corpse was found right beneath the "For Sale" sign on the front door of the church. The police assumed it to have been the work of some capricious punk. But in her heart Hajra knew that the evening on which the racists had raised hell, Ghulam Mohammad had left the house with his cheque-book in his pocket in order to complete the deal on the church; and at the same time his son Nazeer had stuffed a gun into his hip-pocket and as he had left, he had given his father's cap a kick right out of the room.

Originally translated from the Urdu
by Atiya Shah

Sources

The following notes are intended to identify only those translations that have been published previously.

Razia Fasih Ahmed. "Paper is Money", *The Man with the Mask*, Pakistan Urdu Academy, 1994.

Jamila Hashmi. "Banishment" in Ahmed Ali (ed.), *Selected Short Stories from Pakistan Academy of Letters*, Islamabad, Pakistan Academy of Letters.

Khalida Hussain. "Millipede" translated by Muhammad Muar Memon & Wayne Husted from Muhammad Muar Memon (ed.), *The Colour of Nothingness*, Harmondsworth, Penguin Books, 1992.

Mumtaz Shireen. "Descent" in Asif Farrukhi (ed.), *Footfalls Echo*, Karachi, 1997.

Glossary

Abbaji/Abbu	father
Ammah/Ami	mother
anna	unit of currency, one sixteenth of a rupee, before the decimal system was introduced
Apa	elder sister
Asar	afternoon prayer
Baba	father
Badi Ma	grandmother
Bahu	daughter-in-law
beedi	tobacco rolled up in a special kind of leaf; a kind of cigarette
Beti	daughter
Bhai/Bhayya	brother
bibi	a respectable or virtuous woman; also used as a form of address
bindya	a spangle pasted on the forehead
burqa	a long garment, worn by Muslim women for veiling purposes
Chachaji	a form of address to the father's brother
Chachi	wife of father's brother
Chadur	a wrap for covering head and upper part of the body
charpoy	a stringed bed
chilla	meditation or worship in solitude for forty days to obtain spiritual powers

chowkie	a very low stool; the word is also used to denote a ritual
Dasehra	a Hindu festival celerated each year to mark the slaying of Sri Lankan King Rawan who had abducted Lord Rama's wife Sifa during Rama's self-exile
devi	goddess
dholak	a small drum
dupatta	A type of narrow scarf, a couple of metres long, generally made of a light gauzy material, worn by women typically to cover the head, shoulders and breasts.
guru	spiritual teacher
hakeem	a physician practising Muslim-Vedic-Greek medicine
jarga	jury consisting of community elders
kafi	a form of poetry, popular among the mystic poets of the Subcontinent
kahari	maid-servant
kamarband	a long string (usually woven) used as a waist-band
Khala	mother's sister
Koran	Holy Book of the Muslims
kurta	a long shirt
kutchi abadi	temporary settlement
mantra	an incantation
Maulvi Sahib	a teacher and preacher of the theory and practice of Islam
mehri	maid-servant
muezzin	one who calls the Muslims for prayers
naakh	name of a fruit tree
nazar	an offering
neem	margosa tree
paisa	unit of currency (one hundredth of a rupee)

peepal	name of a tree
peer	a spiritual guide
Pehlawan	a wrestler; someone strong and sturdy
rani	queen
Rawan	demon of Hindu mythology
roti	bread, cooked on a hot plate or in a clay oven
seer	a measurement of weight equivalent to approximately one kilogram
Sindhi	belonging to Sindh
tauba	promising Allah never to sin again
Zahida Parveen	name of a well-known singer of Pakistan